# For the Love of Lilah

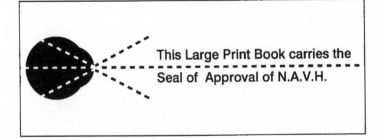

This Large Print Book carries the
Seal of Approval of N.A.V.H.

# NORA ROBERTS

## The Calhouns: Lilah
### *For the Love of Lilah*

**WHEELER**
**PUBLISHING**

Published in 2005 by arrangement with Harlequin Books S.A.

Wheeler Large Print Romance.

The text of this Large Print edition is unabridged.
Other aspects of the book may vary from the original edition.

Set in 16 pt. Plantin by Christina S. Huff.

Printed in the United States on permanent paper.

---

**Library of Congress Cataloging-in-Publication Data**

Roberts, Nora.
    The Calhouns — Lilah : for the love of Lilah / by Nora
Roberts.
        p.   cm. — (Wheeler Publishing large print romance)
    ISBN 1-58724-977-4 (lg. print : hc : alk. paper)
    1. Storms — Fiction.   2. Rescues — Fiction.   3. Large
type books.   I. Title: For the love of Lilah.   II. Title.
III. Wheeler large print romance series.
PS3568.O243F67 2005
813'.54—dc22                                    2005005030

To my great-great-grandmother
Selina MacGruder,
who fell in love unwisely and well.

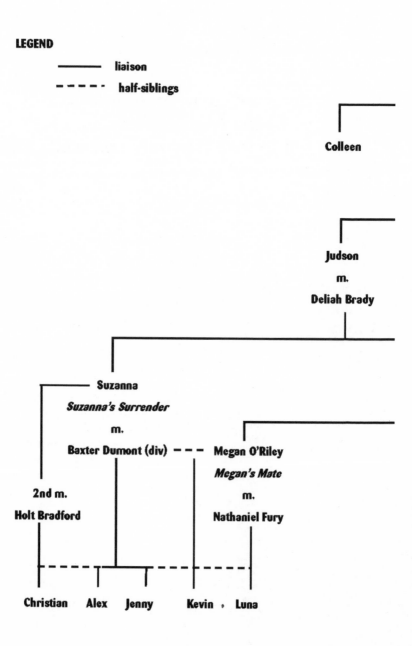

**LEGEND**

—————— liaison

— — — — — half-siblings

Colleen

Judson

m.

Deliah Brady

Suzanna

*Suzanna's Surrender*

m.

Baxter Dumont (div) — — — Megan O'Riley

*Megan's Mate*

2nd m.                                         m.

Holt Bradford                          Nathaniel Fury

Christian    Alex    Jenny    Kevin  ,  Luna

# THE CALHOUNS

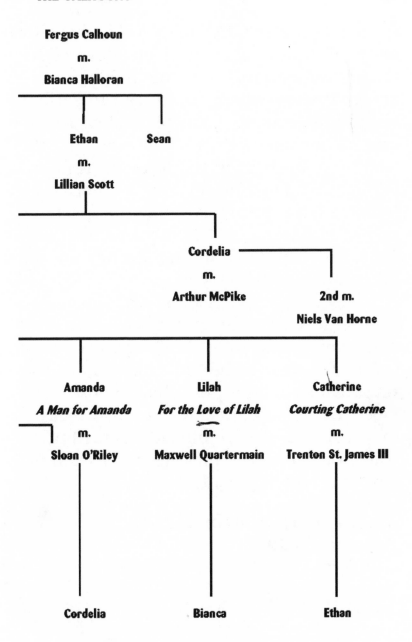

Fergus Calhoun
m.
Bianca Halloran

Ethan        Sean
m.
Lillian Scott

Cordelia
m.
Arthur McPike        2nd m.
                     Niels Van Horne

Amanda              Lilah                   Catherine
*A Man for Amanda*  *For the Love of Lilah*  *Courting Catherine*
m.                  m.                       m.
Sloan O'Riley       Maxwell Quartermain      Trenton St. James III

Cordelia            Bianca                   Ethan

As the Founder/CEO of NAVH, the only national health agency solely devoted to those who, although not totally blind, have an eye disease which could lead to serious visual impairment, I am pleased to recognize Thorndike Press* as one of the leading publishers in the large print field.

Founded in 1954 in San Francisco to prepare large print textbooks for partially seeing children, NAVH became the pioneer and standard setting agency in the preparation of large type.

Today, those publishers who meet our standards carry the prestigious "Seal of Approval" indicating high quality large print. We are delighted that Thorndike Press is one of the publishers whose titles meet these standards. We are also pleased to recognize the significant contribution Thorndike Press is making in this important and growing field.

Lorraine H. Marchi, L.H.D.
Founder/CEO
NAVH

* Thorndike Press encompasses the following imprints: Thorndike, Wheeler, Walker and Large Print Press.

Sweet sister Lilah saved a mysterious stranger from drowning, a man she discovered could touch her heart with the merest glance. But Professor Max Quartermain was a man with secrets — what might he tell . . . *For the Love of Lilah.*

# *Prologue*

Bar Harbor, 1913

*The cliffs call to me. High and fierce and dangerously beautiful, they stand and beckon as seductively as a lover. In the morning, the air was as soft as the clouds that rode the sky to the west. Gulls wheeled and called, a lonely sound, like the distant ring of a buoy that carried up on the wind. It brought an image of a church bell tolling a birth. Or a death.*

*Like a mirage, other islands glinted and winked through the faint mist the sun had yet to burn from the water. Fishermen piloted their sturdy boats from the bay and out to the rolling sea.*

*Even knowing he would not be there, I couldn't stay away.*

*I took the children. It can't be wrong to want to share with them some of the happiness that I always feel when I walk in the wild grass that leads to the tumbled rocks. I held Ethan's hand on one side,*

11

and Colleen's on the other. Nanny gripped little Sean's as he toddled through the grass after a yellow butterfly that fluttered just beyond his questing fingers.

The sound of their laughter — the sweetest sound a mother can hear — lifted through the air. They have such bright and depthless curiosity, such unquestioning trust. As yet, they are untouched by the worries of the world, of uprisings in Mexico, of unrest in Europe. Their world does not include betrayals or guilt or passions that sting the heart. Their needs, so simple, are immediate and have nothing to do with tomorrow. If I could keep them so innocent, so safe and so free, I would. Yet I know that one day they will face all of those churning adult emotions and worries.

But today there were wildflowers to be picked, questions to be answered. And for me, dreams to be dreamed.

There is no doubt that Nanny understands why I walk here. She knows me too well not to see into my heart. She loves me too well to criticize. No one would be more aware than she that there is no love in my marriage. It is, as it has always been, a convenience to Fergus, a duty to me. If not for the children, we would have nothing in common. Even then, I fear he considers them worthwhile possessions, symbols of his success, such as our home in New York, or The Towers, the castlelike house he built for summers on the island. Or myself, the woman he took as wife, one whom he considers attractive enough, well-bred enough to share the Calhoun name, to grace his dinner table or adorn his arm when we walk into the society that is so important to him.

It sounds cold when I write it, yet I cannot pretend there has been warmth in my marriage to Fergus. Certainly there is no passion. I had hoped, when I followed my parents' wishes and married him, that there would be affection, which would deepen into love. But I was very young. There is courtesy, a hollow substitute for emotion.

A year ago perhaps, I could convince myself that I was content. I have a prosperous husband, children I adore, an enviable place in society and a circle of elegant friends. My wardrobe is crowded with beautiful clothes and jewelry. The emeralds Fergus gave me when Ethan was born are fit for a queen. My summer home is magnificent, again suited to royalty with its towers and turrets, its lofty walls papered in silk, its floors gleaming beneath the richest of carpets.

What woman would not be content with all of this? What more could a dutiful wife ask for? Unless she asked for love.

It was love I found along these cliffs, in the artist who stood there, facing the sea, slicing those rocks and raging water onto canvas. Christian, his dark hair blowing in the wind, his gray eyes so dark, so intense, as they studied me. Perhaps if I had not met him I could have gone on pretending to be content. I could have gone on convincing myself that I did not yearn for love or sweet words or a quiet touch in the middle of the night.

Yet I did meet him, and my life has changed. I would not go back to that false contentment for a hundred emerald necklaces. With Christian I have found something so much more precious than all the gold Fergus so cleverly accumulates. It is not something I can hold in my hand or wear around my throat, but something I hold in my heart.

When I meet him on the cliffs, as I will this afternoon, I will not grieve for what we can't have, what we dare not take, but *treasure the hours we've been given. When I feel his arms around me, taste his lips against mine, I'll know that Bianca is the luckiest woman in the world to have been loved so well.*

# Chapter One

A storm was waiting to happen. From the high curving window of the tower, Lilah could see the silver tongue of lightning licking at the black sky to the east. Thunder bellowed, bursting through the gathering clouds to send its drumbeat along the teeth of rock. An answering shudder coursed through her — not of fear, but of excitement.

Something was coming. She could feel it, not just in the thickening of the air but in the primitive beating of her own blood.

When she pressed her hand to the glass, she almost expected her fingers to sizzle, snapped with the power of the building electricity. But the glass was cool and smooth, and as black as the sky.

She smiled a little at the distant rumble of thunder and thought of her great-grandmother. Had Bianca ever stood here, watching a storm build, waiting for it to crash over the house and fill the tower with eerie light? Had she wished that her lover had stood beside her to share the power and the unleashed passion? Of course she had, Lilah thought. What woman wouldn't?

But Bianca had stood here alone, Lilah knew, just as she herself was standing alone now. Perhaps it had been the loneliness, the sheer ache of it, that had driven Bianca to throw herself out of that very window and onto the unforgiving rocks below.

Shaking her head, Lilah took her hand from the glass. She was letting herself get moody again, and it had to stop. Depression and dark thoughts were out of character for a woman who preferred to take life as it came — and who made it a policy to avoid its more strenuous burdens.

Lilah wasn't ashamed of the fact that she would rather sit than stand, would certainly rather walk than run and saw the value of long naps as opposed to exercise for keeping the body and mind in tune.

Not that she wasn't ambitious. It was simply that her ambitions ran to the notion that physical comfort had priority over physical accomplishments.

She didn't care for brooding and was annoyed with herself for falling into the habit over the past few weeks. If anything she should be happy. Her life was moving

17

along at a steady if unhurried pace. Her home and her family, equally important as her own comfort, were safe and whole. In fact, both were expanding along very satisfactory lines.

Her youngest sister, C.C., was back from her honeymoon and glowing like a rose. Amanda, the most practical of the Calhoun sisters, was madly in love and planning her own wedding.

The two men in her sisters' lives met with Lilah's complete approval. Trenton St. James, her new brother-in-law, was a crafty businessman with a soft heart under a meticulously tailored suit. Sloan O'Riley, with his cowboy boots and Oklahoma drawl, had her admiration for digging beneath Amanda's prickly exterior.

Of course, having two of her beloved nieces attached to wonderful men made Aunt Coco delirious with happiness. Lilah laughed a little, thinking how her aunt was certain she'd all but arranged the love affairs herself. Now, naturally, the Calhoun sisters' long-time guardian was itching to provide the same service for Lilah and her older sister Suzanna.

Good luck, Lilah wished her aunt. After a traumatic divorce, and with two young children to care for — not to mention a business to run — Suzanna wasn't likely to cooperate. She'd been badly burned once, and a smart woman didn't let herself get pushed into the fire.

For herself, Lilah had been doing her best to fall in love, to hear that vibrant inner click that came when you knew you'd found the one person in the world who was fated for you. So far, that particular chamber of her heart had been stubbornly silent.

There was time for that, she reminded herself. She was twenty-seven, happy enough in her work, surrounded by family. A few months before, they had nearly lost The Towers, the Calhoun's crumbling and eccentric home that stood on the cliffs overlooking the sea. If it hadn't been for Trent, Lilah might not have been able to stand in the tower room she loved so much and look out at the gathering storm.

So she had her home, her family, a job that interested her and, she reminded herself, a mystery to solve. Great-Grandmama Bianca's emeralds, she thought. Though she had never seen them, she was able to visualize them perfectly just by closing her eyes.

Two dramatic tiers of grass-green stones accented with icy diamonds. The glint of

19

gold in the fancy filigree work. And dripping from the bottom strand, that rich and glowing teardrop emerald. More than its financial or even aesthetic value, it represented to Lilah a direct link with an ancestor who fascinated her, and the hope of eternal love.

The legend said that Bianca, determined to end a loveless marriage, had packed a few of her treasured belongings, including the necklace, into a box. Hoping to find a way to join her lover, she had hidden it. Before she had been able to take it out and start a life with Christian, she had despaired and leaped from the tower window to her death.

A tragic end to a romance, Lilah thought, yet she didn't always feel sad when she thought of it. Bianca's spirit remained in The Towers, and in that high room where Bianca had spent so many hours longing for her lover, Lilah felt close to her.

They would find the emeralds, she promised herself. They were meant to.

It was true enough that the necklace had already caused its problems. The press had learned of its existence and had played endlessly on the hidden-treasure angle. So successfully, Lilah thought now, that the annoyance had gone beyond curious tourists and amateur treasure hunters, and had brought a ruthless thief into their home.

When she thought of how Amanda might have been killed protecting the family's papers, the risk she had taken trying to keep any clue to the emeralds out of the wrong hands, Lilah shuddered. Despite Amanda's heroics, the man who had called himself William Livingston had gotten away with a sackful. Lilah sincerely hoped he found nothing but old recipes and unpaid bills.

William Livingston, alias Peter Mitchell, alias a dozen other names wasn't going to get his greedy hands on the emeralds. Not if the Calhoun women had anything to do about it. As far as Lilah was concerned, that included Bianca, who was as much a part of The Towers as the cracked plaster and creaky boards.

Restless, she moved away from the window. She couldn't say why the emeralds and the woman who had owned them preyed so heavily on her mind tonight. But Lilah was a woman who believed in instinct, in premonition, as naturally as she believed the sun rose in the east.

Tonight, something was coming.

She glanced back toward the window.

The storm was rolling closer, gathering force. She felt a driving need to be outside to meet it.

Max felt his stomach lurch along with the boat. Yacht, he reminded himself. A ^HUNDRED twenty-six-foot beauty with all the comforts of home. Certainly more than his own home, which consisted of a cramped apartment, carelessly furnished, near the campus of Cornell University. The trouble was, the twenty-six-foot beauty was sitting on top of a very cranky Atlantic, and the two seasickness pills in Max's system were no match for it.

He brushed the dark lock of hair away from his brow where, as always, it fell untidily back again. The reeling of the boat sent the brass lamp above his desk dancing. Max did his best to ignore it. He really had to concentrate on his job. American history professors weren't offered fascinating and lucrative summer employment every day. And there was a very good chance he could get a book out of it.

Being hired as researcher for an eccentric millionaire was the fodder of fiction. In this case, it was fact.

As the ship pitched, Max pressed a hand

to his queasy stomach and tried three deep breaths. When that didn't work, he tried concentrating on his good fortune.

The letter from Ellis Caufield had come at a perfect time, just before Max had committed himself to a summer assignment. The offer had been both irresistible and flattering.

In the day-to-day scheme of things, Max didn't consider that he had a reputation. Some well-received articles, a few awards — but that was all within the tight world of academia that Max had happily buried himself in. If he was a good teacher, he felt it was because he received such pleasure from giving both information and appreciation of the past to students so mired in the present.

It had come as a surprise that Caufield, a layman, would have heard of him and would respect him enough to offer him such interesting work.

What was even more exciting than the yacht, the salary and the idea of summering in Bar Harbor, to a man with Maxwell Quartermain's mind-set, was the history in every scrap of paper he'd been assigned to catalogue.

A receipt for a lady's hat, dated 1932. The guest list for a party from 1911. A copy of a repair bill on a 1935 Ford. The handwritten instructions for an herbal remedy for the croup. There were letters written before World War I, newspaper clippings with names like Carnegie and Kennedy, shipping receipts for Chippendale armoires, a Waterford chandelier. Old dance cards, faded recipes.

For a man who spent most of his intellectual life in the past, it was a treasure trove. He would have shifted through each scrap happily for nothing, but Ellis Caufield had contacted him, offering Max more than he made teaching two full semesters.

It was a dream come true. Instead of spending the summer struggling to interest bored students in the cultural and political status of America before the Great War, he was living it. With the money, half of which was already deposited, Max could afford to take a year off from teaching to start the book he'd been longing to write.

Max felt he owed Caufield an enormous debt. A year to indulge himself. It was more than he had ever dared to dream of. Brains had gotten him into Cornell on a scholarship. Brains and hard work had earned him a Ph.D. by the time he'd been twenty-five. For the eight years since then, he'd been slaving, teaching classes, preparing lectures, grading papers, taking the time only to write a few articles.

Now, thanks to Caufield, he would be able to take the time he had never dared to take. He would be able to begin the project he kept secret inside his head and heart.

He wanted to write a novel set in the second decade of the twentieth century. Not just a history lesson or an oratory on the cause and effect of war, but a story of people swept along by history. The kind of people he was growing to know and understand by reading through their old papers.

Caufield had given him that time, the research and the opportunity. And it was all gilded by a summer spent luxuriously on a yacht. It was a pity Max hadn't realized how much his system would resent the motion of the sea.

Particularly a stormy one, he thought, rubbing a hand over his clammy face. He struggled to concentrate, but the faded and tiny print on the papers swam then doubled in front of his eyes and added a vicious headache to the grinding nausea. What he needed was some air, he told himself. A good blast of fresh air. Though he knew Caufield preferred him to stay below with his research during the evenings, Max figured his employer would prefer him healthy rather than curled up moaning on his bed.

Rising, he did moan a little, his stomach heaving with the next wave. He could almost feel his skin turn green. Air, definitely. Max stumbled from the cabin, wondering if he would ever find his sea legs. After a week, he'd thought he'd been doing fairly well, but with the first taste of rough weather, he was wobbly.

It was a good thing he hadn't — as he sometimes liked to imagine — sailed on the *Mayflower*. He never would have made it to Plymouth Rock.

Bracing a hand on the mahogany paneling, he hobbled down the pitching corridor toward the stairs that led above deck.

Caufield's cabin door was open. Max, who would never stoop to eavesdropping, paused only to give his stomach a moment to settle. He heard his employer speaking to the captain. As the dizziness cleared from Max's head, he realized they were not speaking about the weather or plotting a course.

"I don't intend to lose the necklace," Caufield said impatiently. "I've gone to a lot of trouble, and expense, already."

The captain's answer was equally taut. "I

don't see why you brought Quartermain in. If he realizes why you want those papers, and how you got them, he'll be trouble."

"He won't find out. As far as the good professor is concerned, they belong to my family. And I am rich enough, eccentric enough, to want them preserved."

"If he hears something —"

"Hears something?" Caufield interrupted with a laugh. "He's so buried in the past he doesn't hear his own name. Why do you think I chose him? I do my homework, Hawkins, and I researched Quartermain thoroughly. He's an academic fossil with more brains than wit, and is curious only about what happened in the past. Current events, such as armed robbery and the Calhoun emeralds are beyond him."

In the corridor, Max remained still and silent, the physical illness warring with sick suspicion. *Armed robbery.* The two words reeled in his head.

"We'd be better off in New York," Hawkins complained. "I cased out the Wallingford job while you were kicking your heels last month. We could have the old lady's diamonds inside of a week."

"The diamonds will wait." Caufield's voice hardened. "I want the emeralds, and

27

I intend to have them. I've been twenty years in the business of stealing, Hawkins, and I know that only once in a lifetime does a man have the chance for something this big."

"The diamonds —"

"Are stones." Now the voice was caressing and perhaps a little mad. "The emeralds are a legend. They're going to be mine. Whatever it takes."

Max stood frozen outside of the stateroom. The clammy illness roiling inside of his stomach was iced with shock. He hadn't a clue what they were talking about or how to put it together. But one thing was obvious — he was being used by a thief, and there was something other than history in the papers he'd been hired to research.

The fanaticism in Caufield's voice hadn't escaped him, nor had the suppressed violence in Hawkins's. And fanaticism had proved itself throughout history to be a most dangerous weapon. His only defense against it was knowledge.

He had to get the papers, get them and find a way off the boat and to the police. Though whatever he could tell them wouldn't make sense. He stepped back, hoping he could clear his thoughts by the time he got to his stateroom. A wicked wave had the boat lurching and Max pitching through the open doorway.

"Dr. Quartermain." Gripping the sides of his desk, Caufield lifted a brow. "Well, it seems as though you're in the wrong place at the wrong time."

Max grasped the doorjamb as he stumbled back, cursing the unsteady deck beneath his feet. "I — wanted some air."

"He heard every damn word," the captain muttered.

"I'm aware of that, Hawkins. The professor isn't blessed with a poker face. Well then," he began as he slid a drawer open, "we'll simply alter the plans a bit. I'm afraid you won't be granted any shore leave during our stay in Bar Harbor, Doctor." He pulled out a chrome-plated revolver. "An inconvenience, I know, but I'm sure you'll find your cabin more than adequate for your needs while you work. Hawkins, take him back and lock him in."

A crash of thunder vibrated the boat. It was all Max needed to uproot his legs. As the boat swayed, he rushed back into the corridor. Pulling himself along by the handrail, he fought the motion of the boat. The shouts behind him were lost as he came above deck into the howl of the wind.

A spray of saltwater dashed across his face, blinding him for a moment as he frantically looked for a means of escape. Lightning cracked the black sky, showing him the single stab of light, the pitching seas, the distant, angry rocks and the vague shadow of land. The next roll nearly felled him, but he managed through a combination of luck and sheer will to stay upright. Driven by instinct, he ran, feet sliding on the wet deck. In the next flash of lightning he saw one of the mates glance over from his post. The man called something and gestured, but Max spun around on the slippery deck and ran on.

He tried to think, but his head was too crowded, too jumbled. The storm, the pitching boat, the image of that glinting gun. It was like being caught in someone else's nightmare. He was a history professor, a man who lived in books, rarely surfacing long enough to remember if he'd eaten or picked up his cleaning. He was, he knew, terminally boring, calmly pacing himself on the academic treadmill as he had done all of his life. Surely he couldn't be on a yacht in the Atlantic being chased by armed thieves.

"Doctor."

His erstwhile employer's voice was close

enough to cause Max to turn around. The gun being held less than five feet away reminded Max that some nightmares were real. Slowly he backed up until he rammed into the guardrail. There was nowhere left to run.

"I know this is an inconvenience," Caufield said, "but I think it would be wise if you went back to your cabin." A bolt of lightning emphasized the point. "The storm should be short, but quite severe. We wouldn't want you to . . . fall overboard."

"You're a thief."

"Yes." Legs braced against the rolling deck, Caufield smiled. He was enjoying himself — the wind, the electric air, the white face of the prey he had cornered. "And now that I can be more frank about just what I want you to look for, our work should go much more quickly. Come now, Doctor, use that celebrated brain of yours."

From the corner of his eye, Max saw that Hawkins was closing in from the other side, as steady on the heeling deck as a mountain goat on a beaten path. In a moment, they would have him. Once they did, he was quite certain he would never see the inside of a classroom again.

With an instinct for survival that had never been tested, he swung over the rail. He heard another crack of thunder, felt a burning along his temple, then plunged blindly beneath the dark, swirling water.

Lilah had driven down, following the winding road to the base of the cliff. The wind had picked up, was shrieking now as she stepped out of her car and let it stream through her hair. She didn't know why she'd felt compelled to come here, to stand alone on this narrow and rocky stretch of beach to face the storm.

But she had come, and the exhilaration streamed into her, racing just under her skin, speeding up her heart. When she laughed, the sound hung on the wind then echoed away. Power and passion exploded around her in a war she could delight in.

Water fumed against the rock, spouting up, spraying her. There was an icy feel to it that made her shiver, but she didn't draw back. Instead she closed her eyes for a moment, lifted her face and absorbed it.

The noise was huge, wildly primitive. Above, closer now, the storm threatened. Big and bad and boisterous. The rain, so heavy in the air you could taste it, held up, but the lightning took command, spearing the sky, ripping through the dark while the boom of thunder competed with the crash of water and wind.

She felt as though she were alone in a violent painting, but there was no sense of loneliness and certainly none of fear. It was anticipation that prickled along her skin, just as a passion as dark as the storm's beat in her blood.

Something, she thought again as she lifted her face to the wind, was coming.

If it hadn't been for the lightning, she wouldn't have seen him. At first she watched the dark shape in the darker water and wondered if a dolphin had swum too close to the rocks. Curious, she walked over the shale, dragging her hair away from the greedy fingers of wind.

Not a dolphin, she realized with a clutch of panic. A man. Too stunned to move, she watched him go under. Surely she'd imagined it, she told herself. She was just caught up in the storm, the mystery of it, the sense of immediacy. It was crazy to think she'd seen someone fighting the waves in this lonely and violent span of water.

But when the figure appeared again, floundering, Lilah was kicking off her sandals and racing into the icy black water.

His energy was flagging. Though he'd managed to pry off his shoes, his legs felt abominably heavy. He'd always been a strong swimmer. It was the only sport he had had any talent for. But the sea was a great deal stronger. It carried him along now rather than his own arms and legs. It dragged him under as it chose, then teasingly released him as he struggled to break free for one more gulp of air.

He couldn't even remember why he was fighting. The cold that had long since numbed his body granted the same favor to his brain. His thrashing movements were merely automatic now and growing steadily weaker. It was the sea that guided him, that trapped him, that would, he was coming to accept, kill him.

The next wave battered him, and exhausted, he let it take him under. He only hoped he would drown before he bashed into the rocks.

He felt something wrap around his neck and, with the last of his strength, pushed at it. Some wild thought of sea snakes or grasping weeds had him struggling. Then his face was above the surface again, his burning lungs sucking air. Dimly he saw a face close to his own. Pale, stunningly beautiful. A glory of dark, wet hair floated around him.

"Just hang on," she shouted at him. "We'll be all right."

She was pulling him toward shore, fighting the backwash of wave. Hallucinating, Max thought. He had to be hallucinating to imagine a beautiful woman coming to his aid a moment before he died. But the possibility of a miracle kicked into his fading sense of survival, and he began to work with her.

The waves slammed into them, dragging them back a foot for every two exhausting feet of progress they made. Overhead the sky opened to pour out a lashing rain. She was shouting something again, but all he could hear was the dull buzzing in his own head.

He decided he must already be dead. There certainly was no more pain. All he could see was her face, the glow of her eyes, the water-slicked lashes. A man could do worse than to die with that image in his mind.

But her eyes were bright with anger, electric with it. She wanted help, he realized. She needed help. Instinctively he put an arm around her waist so that they were towing each other.

He lost track of the times they went under, of the times one would pull the other up again. When he saw the jutting rocks, fangs spearing up through the swirling black, he turned his weary body without thought to shield hers. An angry wave flicked them waist high out of the water, as easily as a finger flicks an ant from a stone.

His shoulder slammed against rock, but he barely felt it. Then there was the grit of sand beneath his knees, biting into flesh. The water fought to suck them back, but they crawled onto the rocky shore.

The initial sickness was hideous, racking through him until he was certain his body would simply break apart. When the worst of it passed, he rolled, coughing, onto his back. The sky wheeled overhead, black, then brilliant. The face was above his again, close. A hand moved gently over his brow.

"You made it, sailor."

He only stared. She was eerily beautiful, like something he might have conjured if he'd had enough imagination. In the flickering lightning he could see her hair was a rich, golden red. She had acres of it. It flowed around her face, down her shoulders, onto his chest. Her eyes were the mystical green of a calm sea. As the water ran from her onto him, he reached up to touch her face, certain they would pass through the image. But he felt her skin, cold, wet and soft as spring rain.

"Real." His voice was a husky croak. "You're real."

"Damn right." She smiled, then cupping his face in her hands, laughed. "You're alive. We're both alive." And kissed him. Deeply, lavishly, until his head spun with it. There was more laughter beneath the kiss. He heard the joy in it, but not the simple relief.

When he looked at her again, she was blurring, that ethereal face fading until all he could see were those incredible, glowing eyes.

"I never believed in mermaids," he murmured before he lost consciousness.

# Chapter Two

"Poor man." Coco, splendid in a flowing purple caftan, hovered beside the bed. She kept her voice low and watched, eagle eyed, as Lilah bandaged the shallow crease on their unconscious guest's temple. "What in the world could have happened to him?"

"We'll have to wait and ask." Her fingers gentle, Lilah studied the pale face on the pillow. Early thirties, she guessed. No tan, though it was mid-June. The indoor type, she decided, despite the fact that he had fairly good muscles. His body was well toned, if a bit on the lanky side — the weight of it had given her more than a little trouble when she'd dragged him to the car. His face was lean, a little long, nicely bony. Intellectual, she thought. The mouth was certainly engaging. Rather poetic, like the pallor. Though his eyes were closed now, she knew they were blue. His hair, nearly dry, was full of sand and long and thick. It was dark and straight, like his lashes.

"I called the doctor," Amanda said as

she hurried into the bedroom. Her fingers tapped on the footboard as she frowned down at the patient. "He says we should bring him into Emergency."

Lilah looked up as the lightning struck close to the house and the rain slashed against the windows. "I don't want to take him out in this unless we have to."

"I think she's right." Suzanna stood on the other side of the bed. "I also think Lilah should have a hot bath and lie down."

"I'm fine." At the moment she was wrapped in a chenille robe, warmed by that and a healthy dose of brandy. In any case, she was feeling much too proprietary about her charge to turn him over.

"Crazy is what you are." C.C. massaged Lilah's neck as she lectured her. "Diving into the ocean in the middle of a storm."

"I guess I could've let him drown." Lilah patted C.C.'s hand. "Where's Trent?"

C.C. sighed as she thought of her new husband. "He and Sloan are making sure the new construction's protected. The rain's coming down pretty hard and they were worried about water damage."

"I think I should make some chicken soup." Coco, maternal instincts humming, studied the patient again. "That's just what he needs when he wakes up."

He was already waking up, groggily. He heard the distant and lovely sound of women's voices. Low pitched, smooth, soothing. Like music, it lulled him in and out of dreams. When he turned his head, Max felt the gentle feminine touch on his brow. Slowly, he opened eyes still burning from salt water. The dimly lit room blurred, tilted, then slid into soft focus.

There were five of them, he noted dreamily. Five stupendous examples of womanhood. On one side of the bed was a blonde, poetically lovely, eyes filled with concern. At the foot was a tall, trim brunette who seemed both impatient and sympathetic. An older woman with smoky-blond hair and a regal figure beamed at him. A green-eyed, raven-haired Amazon tilted her head and smiled more cautiously.

Then there was his mermaid, sitting beside him in a white robe, her fabulous hair falling in wild curls to her waist. He must have made some gesture, for they all came a little closer, as if to offer comfort. The mermaid's hand covered his.

"I guess this is heaven," he managed through a dry throat. "It's worth dying for."

With a laugh, Lilah squeezed his fingers. "Nice thought, but this is Maine," she corrected. Lifting a cup, she eased brandy-laced tea through his lips. "You're not dead, just tired."

"Chicken soup." Coco stepped forward to tidy the blanket over him. She was vain enough to take an instant liking to him for his waking statement. "Doesn't that sound good, dear?"

"Yes." The thought of something warm sliding down his aching throat sounded glorious. Though it hurt to swallow, he took another greedy gulp of tea. "Who are you?"

"We're the Calhouns," Amanda said from the foot of the bed. "Welcome to The Towers."

Calhouns. There was something familiar about the name, but it drifted away, like the dream of drowning. "I'm sorry, I don't know how I got here."

"Lilah brought you," C.C. told him. "She —"

"You had an accident," Lilah interrupted her sister, and smiled at him. "Don't worry about it right now. You should rest."

It wasn't a question of should, but must. He could already feel himself drifting away. "You're Lilah," he said groggily. As he drifted to sleep, he repeated the name, finding it lyrical enough to dream on.

41

"How's the lifeguard this morning?"

Lilah turned from the stove to look at Sloan, Amanda's fiancé. At six-four, he filled the doorway, was so blatantly male — and relaxed with it — she had to smile.

"I guess I earned my first merit badge."

"Next time try making a pot holder." After crossing the room, he kissed the top of her head. "We wouldn't want to lose you."

"I figure jumping into a stormy sea once in my life is enough." With a little sigh, she leaned against him. "I was petrified."

"What the hell were you doing down there with a storm coming?"

"Just one of those things." She shrugged, then went back to fixing tea. For now, she preferred to keep the sensation of being sent to the beach to herself.

"Did you find out who he is?"

"No, not yet. He didn't have a wallet on him, and since he was in pretty rough shape last night, I didn't want to badger him." She glanced up, caught Sloan's expression and shook her head. "Come on, big guy, he's hardly dangerous. If he was looking for a way into the house to have a shot at finding the necklace, he could have taken an easier route than drowning."

He was forced to agree, but after having Amanda shot at, he didn't want to take chances. "Whoever he is, I think you should move him to the hospital."

"Let me worry about it." She began to arrange plates and cups on a tray. "He's all right, Sloan. Trust me?"

Frowning, he put a hand on hers before she could lift the tray. "Vibes?"

"Absolutely." With a laugh, she tossed back her hair. "Now, I'm going to take Mr. X some breakfast. Why don't you get back to knocking down walls in the west wing?"

"We're putting a few up today." And because he did trust her, he relaxed a little. "Aren't you going to be late for work?"

"I took the day off to play Florence Nightingale." She slapped his hand away from the saucer of toast. "Go be an architect."

Balancing the tray, she left Sloan to start down the hallway. The main floor of The Towers was a hodgepodge of rooms with towering ceilings and cracked plaster. In its heyday, it had been a showplace, an elaborate summer home built by Fergus Calhoun in 1904. It had been his symbol of status with gleaming paneling, crystal doorknobs, intricate murals.

43

Now the roof leaked in too many places to count, the plumbing rattled and the plaster flaked. Like her sisters, Lilah adored every inch of chipped molding. It had been her home, her only home, and held memories of the parents she had lost fifteen years before.

At the top of the curving stairs, she paused. Muffled with distance came the energetic sound of hammering. The west wing was getting a much needed face-lift. Between Sloan and Trent, The Towers would recapture at least part of its former glory. Lilah liked the idea and, as a woman who considered napping a favored pastime, enjoyed the sound of busy hands.

He was still sleeping when she walked into the room. She knew he had barely stirred through the night because she had stretched out on the foot of the bed, reluctant to leave him, and had slept there, patchily, until morning.

Quietly Lilah set the tray on the bureau and moved over to open the terrace doors. Warm and fragrant air glided in. Unable to resist, she stepped out to let it revitalize her. The sunlight sparkled on the wet grass, glittered on the petals of shell-pink peonies still heavy-headed from rain. Clematis, their saucer-sized blossoms royally blue, spiraled on one of the white trellises in a race with the climbing roses.

From the waist-high terrace wall, she could see the glint of the deep blue water of the bay and the greener, less serene, surface of the Atlantic. It hardly seemed possible that she had been in the water just last night, grasping a stranger and fighting for life. But muscles, unaccustomed to the exercise, ached enough to bring the moment, and the terror, back.

She preferred concentrating on the morning, the generous laziness of it. Made tiny as a toy by the distance, one of the tourist boats streamed by, filled with people clutching cameras and children, hoping to see a whale.

It was June, and the summer people poured into Bar Harbor to sail, to shop, to sun. They would gobble up lobster rolls, haunt the ice cream and T-shirt shops and pack the streets, searching for the perfect souvenir. To them it was a resort. To Lilah, it was home.

She watched a three-masted schooner head out to sea and allowed herself to dream a little before going back inside.

He was dreaming. Part of his mind recognized it as a dream, but his stomach muscles still fisted, and his pulse rate increased. He was alone in an angry black sea, fighting to make his arms and legs swim through the rising waves. They dragged at him, pulling him under into that blind, airless world. His lungs strained. His own heartbeat roared in his head.

His disorientation was complete — black sea below, black sky above. There was a hideous throbbing in his temple, a terrifying numbness in his limbs. He sank, floating down, fathoms deep. Then she was there, her red hair flowing around her, twining around lovely white breasts, down a slender torso. Her eyes were a soft, mystical green. She spoke his name, and there was a laugh in her voice — and an invitation in the laugh. Slowly, gracefully as a dancer, she held out her arms to him, folding him in. He tasted salt and sex on her lips as she closed them over his.

With a groan, he came regretfully awake. There was pain now, ripe and throbbing in his shoulder, sharp and horrible in his head. His thought patterns skidded away from him. Concentrating, he worked his way above the pain, focusing first on a high, coffered ceiling laced with cracks. He shifted a little, acutely aware that every muscle in his body hurt.

The room was enormous — or perhaps it seemed so because it was so scantily furnished. But what furnishings. There was a huge antique armoire with intricately carved doors. The single chair was undoubtedly Louis Quinze, and the dusty nightstand Hepplewhite. The mattress he lay on sagged, but the footboard was Georgian.

Struggling up to brace on his elbows, he saw Lilah standing in the open terrace doors. The breeze was fluttering those long cables of hair. He swallowed. At least he knew she wasn't a mermaid. She had legs. Lord, she had legs — right up to her eyes. She wore flowered shorts, a plain blue T-shirt and a smile.

"So, you're awake." She came to him and, competent as a mother, laid a hand on his brow. His tongue dried up. "No fever. You're lucky."

"Yeah."

Her smile widened. "Hungry?"

There was definitely a hole in the pit of his stomach. "Yeah." He wondered if he'd ever be able to get more than one word out around her. At the moment he was lecturing himself for having imagined her

47

naked when she'd risked her life to save his. "Your name's Lilah."

"That's right." She walked over to fetch the tray. "I wasn't sure you'd remember anything from last night."

Pain capered through him so that he gritted his teeth against it and struggled to keep his voice even. "I remember five beautiful women. I thought I was in heaven."

She laughed and, setting the tray at the foot of the bed, came to rearrange his pillows. "My three sisters and my aunt. Here, can you sit up a little?"

When her hand slid down his back to brace him, he realized he was naked. Completely. "Ah . . ."

"Don't worry, I won't peek. Yet." She laughed again, leaving him flustered. "Your clothes were drenched — I think the shirt's a lost cause. Relax," she told him as she set the tray on his lap. "My brother-in-law and future brother-in-law got you into bed."

"Oh." It looked as though he was back to single syllables.

"Try the tea," she suggested. "You probably swallowed a gallon of sea water, so I'll bet your throat's raw." She saw the intense concentration in his eyes and the nagging pain behind it. "Headache?"

"Vicious."

"I'll be back." She left him, trailing some potently exotic scent in her wake.

Max used the time alone to build back what little strength he had. He hated being weak — a leftover obsession from childhood when he'd been puny and asthmatic. His father had given up in disgust on building his only and disappointing son into a football star. Though he knew it was illogical, sickness brought back unhappy memories of childhood.

Because he'd always considered his mind stronger than his body, he used it now to block the pain.

Moments later, she was back with an aspirin and witch hazel. "Take a couple of these. After you eat, I can drive you into the hospital."

"Hospital?"

"You might want to have a doctor take a look."

"No." He swallowed the pills. "I don't think so."

"Up to you." She sat on the bed to study him, one leg lazily swinging to some inner tune.

Never in his life had he been so sexually aware of a woman — of the texture of her skin, the subtle tones of it, the shape of her body, her eyes, her mouth. The assault on his senses left him uneasy and baffled. He'd nearly drowned, he reminded himself. Now all he could think about was getting his hands on the woman who'd saved him. Saved his life, he remembered.

"I haven't even thanked you."

"I figured you'd get around to it. Try those eggs before they get any colder. You need food."

Obediently he scooped some up. "Can you tell me what happened?"

"From the time I came into it." Relaxed, she brushed her hair behind her shoulder and settled more comfortably on the bed. "I drove down to the beach. Impulse," she said with a lazy movement of her shoulders. "I'd been watching the storm build from the tower."

"The tower?"

"Here, in the house," she explained. "I got the urge to go down, watch it roll in from sea. Then I saw you." In a careless gesture, she brushed the hair back from his brow. "You were in trouble, so I went in. We sort of pulled each other to shore."

"I remember. You kissed me."

Her lips curved. "I figured we both deserved it." She touched a gentle hand to the bruise spreading on his shoulder. "You hit the rocks. What were you doing out there?"

"I . . ." He closed his eyes to try to clear his fuzzy brain. The effort had sweat pearling on his brow. "I'm not sure."

"Okay, why don't we start with your name?"

"My name?" He opened his eyes to give her a blank look. "Don't you know?"

"We didn't have the chance to introduce ourselves formally. Lilah Calhoun," she said, and offered a hand.

"Quartermain." He accepted her hand, relieved that much was clear. "Maxwell Quartermain."

"Drink some more tea, Max. Ginseng's good for you." Taking the witch hazel, she began to rub it gently over the bruise. "What do you do?"

"I'm, ah, a history professor at Cornell." Her fingers eased the ache in his shoulder and cajoled him into relaxing.

"Tell me about Maxwell Quartermain." She wanted to take his mind off the pain, to see him relax into sleep again. "Where are you from?"

"I grew up in Indiana . . ." Her fingers slid up to his neck to unknot muscles.

"Farm boy?"

"No." He sighed as the tension eased and made her smile. "My parents ran a market. I used to help out after school and over the summer."

"Did you like it?"

His eyes were growing heavy. "It was all right. It gave me plenty of time to study. Annoyed my father — always had my face in a book. He didn't understand. I skipped a couple grades and got into Cornell."

"Scholarship?" she assumed.

"Hmm. Got my doctorate." The words were slurred and weighty. "Do you know how much man accomplished between 1870 and 1970?"

"Amazing."

"Absolutely." He was nearly asleep, coaxed into comfort by her quiet voice and gentle hands. "I'd like to have been alive in 1910."

"Maybe you were." She smiled, amused and charmed. "Take a nap, Max."

When he awakened again, he was alone. But he had a dozen throbbing aches to keep him company. He noted that she had left the aspirin and a carafe of water beside the bed, and gratefully swallowed pills.

When that small chore exhausted him, he leaned back to catch his breath. The sunlight was bright, streaming through the open terrace doors with fresh sea air. He'd lost his sense of time, and though it was tempting just to lie back and shut his eyes again, he needed to take back some sort of control.

Maybe she'd read his mind, he thought as he saw his pants and someone else's shirt neatly folded at the foot of the bed. He rose creakily, like an old man with brittle bones and aching muscles. His body sang a melody of pain as he picked up the clothes and peeked through a side door. He eyed the claw-footed tub and chrome shower works with pleasure.

The pipes thudded when he turned on the spray, and so did his muscles as the water beat against his skin. But ten minutes later, he felt almost alive.

It wasn't easy to dry off — even that simple task had his limbs singing. Not sure the news would be good, he wiped the mist from the mirror to study his face.

Beneath the stubble of beard, his skin was white and drawn. Flowering out from the bandage at his temple was a purpling bruise. He already knew there were plenty more blooming on his body. As a result of salt water, his eyes were a patriotic red, white and blue. Though he'd never considered himself a vain man — his looks had always struck him as dead average — he turned away from the mirror.

Wincing and groaning and swearing under his breath, he struggled into the clothes.

The shirt fit fairly well. Better, in fact, than many of his own. Shopping intimidated him — rather salesclerks intimidated him with their bright, impatient smiles. Most of the time Max shopped out of catalogues and took what came.

Glancing down at his bare feet, Max admitted that he'd have to go shopping for shoes — and soon.

Moving slowly, he walked out onto the terrace. The sunlight stung his eyes, but the breezy, moist air felt like heaven. And the view . . . For a moment he could only stop and stare, hardly even breathing. Water and rock and flowers. It was like being on top of the world and looking down at a small and perfect slice of the planet. The colors were vibrant — sapphire, emerald, the ruby red of roses, the pristine white of sails pregnant with wind. There was no sound but the rumble of the sea and then, far off, the musical gong of a buoy. He could smell hot summer flowers and the cool tang of the ocean.

With his hand braced on the wall, he

began to walk. He didn't know which direction he should take, so wandered aimlessly and with no little effort. Once, when dizziness overtook him, he was forced to stop, shut his eyes and breathe his way through it.

When he came to a set of stairs leading up, he opted to climb them. His legs were wobbly, and he could already feel fatigue tugging at him. It was pride as much as curiosity that had him continuing.

The house was built of granite, a sober and sturdy stone that did nothing to take away from the fancy of the architecture. Max felt as though he were exploring the circumference of a castle, some stubborn bulwark of early history that had taken its place upon the cliffs and held it for generations.

Then he heard the anachronistic buzz of a power saw and a man's casual oath. Walking closer, he recognized the busy noises of construction in progress — the slap of hammer on wood, the tinny music from a portable radio, the whirl of drills. When his path was blocked by sawhorses, lumber and tarps, he knew he'd found the source.

A man stepped out of another set of terrace doors. Reddish-blond hair was tousled around a tanned face. He squinted at Max, then hooked his thumbs in his pockets. "Up and around, I see."

"More or less."

The guy looked as if he'd been kicked by a team of mules, Sloan thought. His face was dead white, his eyes bruised, his skin sheened with the sweat of effort. He was holding himself upright through sheer stubbornness. It made it tough to hold on to suspicions.

"Sloan O'Riley," he said, and offered a hand.

"Maxwell Quartermain."

"So I hear. Lilah says you're a history professor. Taking a vacation?"

"No." Max's brow furrowed. "No, I don't think so."

It wasn't evasion Sloan saw in his eyes, but puzzlement, laced with frustration. "Guess you're still a little rattled."

"I guess." Absently he reached up to touch the bandage at his temple. "I was on a boat," he murmured, straining to visualize it. "Working." On what? "The water was pretty rough. I wanted to go on deck, get some air . . ." Standing at the rail, deck heaving. Panic. "I think I fell —" jumped, was thrown "— I must have fallen overboard."

"Funny nobody reported it."

"Sloan, leave the man alone. Does he look like an international jewel thief?" Lilah strolled lazily up the steps, a short-haired black dog at her heels. The dog jumped at Sloan, tripped, righted himself and managed to get his front paws settled on the knees of Sloan's jeans.

"I wondered where you'd wandered off to," Lilah continued, and cupped a hand under Max's chin to examine his face. "You look a little better," she decided as the dog started to sniff at Max's bare toes. "That's Fred," she told him. "He only bites criminals."

"Oh. Good."

"Since you have his seal of approval, why don't you come down? You can sit in the sun and have some lunch."

He would dearly love to sit, he realized and let Lilah lead him away. "Is this really your house?"

"Hearth and home. My great-grandfather built it just after the turn of the century. Look out for Fred." The dog dashed between them, stepped on his own ear and yelped. Max, who'd gone through a long clumsy stage himself, felt immediate sympathy. "We're thinking of giving him ballet lessons," she said as the dog struggled back to his feet. Noting the blank look on Max's face, she patted his cheek. "I think you could use some of Aunt Coco's chicken soup."

She made him sit and kept an eye on him while he ate. Her protective instincts were usually reserved for family or small, wounded birds. But something about the man tugged at her. He seemed so out of his element, she thought. And helpless with it.

Something was going on behind those big blue eyes, she thought. Something beyond the fatigue. She could almost see him struggle to put one mental foot in front of the other.

He began to think that the soup had saved his life as surely as Lilah had. It slid warm and vital into his system. "I fell out of a boat," he said abruptly.

"That would explain it."

"I don't know what I was doing on a boat, exactly."

In the chair beside him she brought up her limber legs to settle in the lotus position. "Taking a vacation?"

"No." His brow furrowed. "No, I don't take vacations."

"Why not?" She reached over to take one of the crackers from his plate. She wore a trio of glittering rings on her hand.

"Work."

"School's out," she said with a lazy stretch.

"I always teach summer courses. Except . . ." Something was tapping at the edges of his brain, tauntingly. "I was going to do something else this summer. A research project. And I was going to start a book."

"A book, really?" She savored the cracker as if it were laced with caviar. He had to admire her basic, sensual enjoyment. "What kind?"

Her words jerked him back. He'd never told anyone about his plans to write. No one who knew him would have believed that studious, steady-as-she-goes Quartermain dreamed of being a novelist. "It's just something I've been thinking of for a while, but I had a chance to work on this project . . . a family history."

"Well, that would suit you. I was a terrible student. Lazy," she said with a smile in her eyes. "I can't imagine anyone wanting to make a career out of a classroom. Do you like it?"

It wasn't a matter of liking it. It was what he did. "I'm good at it." Yes, he realized, he was good at it. His students learned — some more than others. His lectures were well attended and well received.

"That's not the same thing. Can I see your hand?"

"My what?"

"Your hand," she repeated, and took it, turning it palm up. "Hmm."

"What are you doing?" For a heady moment, he thought she would press her lips to it.

"Looking at your palm. More intelligence than intuitiveness. Or maybe you just trust your brains more than your instincts."

Staring at the top of her bent head, he gave a nervous laugh. "You don't really believe in that sort of thing. Palm reading."

"Of course — but it's not just the lines, it's the feeling." She glanced up briefly with a smile that was at once languid and electric. "You have very nice hands. Look here." She skimmed a finger along his palm and had him swallowing. "You've got a long life ahead of you, but see this break? Near-death experience."

"You're making it up."

"They're your lines," she reminded him. "A good imagination. I think you'll write that book — but you'll have to work on that self-confidence."

She looked up again, a trace of sympathy on her face. "Rough childhood?"

"Yes — no." Embarrassed, he cleared his throat. "No more than anyone's, I imagine."

She lifted a brow, but let it pass. "Well, you're a big boy now." In one of her casual moves, she slid her hair back then studied his hand again. "Yes, see, this represents careers, and there's a branch off this way. Things have been very comfortable for you professionally — you've hoed yourself a nice little rut — but this other line spears off. Could be that literary effort. You'll have to make the choice."

"I really don't think —"

"Sure you do. You've been thinking about it for years. Now here's the Mound of Venus. Hmm. You're a very sensual man." Her gaze flicked up to his again. "And a very thorough lover."

He couldn't take his eyes off her mouth. It was full, unpainted and curved teasingly. Kissing her would be like sinking into a dream — the dark and erotic kind. And if a man survived it, he would pray never to wake up.

She felt something creep in over her amusement. Something unexpected and arousing. It was the way he looked at her, she thought. With such complete absorption. As though she were the only woman in the world — certainly the only one who mattered.

There couldn't be a female alive who wouldn't weaken a bit under that look.

For the first time in her life she felt off balance with a man. She was used to having the controls, of setting the tone in her own unstudied way. From the time she'd understood that boys were different from girls, she had used the power she'd been born with to guide members of the opposite sex down a path of her own choosing.

Yet he was throwing her off with a look.

Struggling for a casualness that had always come easily, she started to release his hand. Max surprised them both by turning his over to grip hers.

"You are," he said slowly, "the most beautiful woman I've ever seen."

It was a standard line, even a cliché, and shouldn't have had her heart leaping. She made herself smile as she drew away. "Don't get out much, do you, Professor?"

There was a flicker of annoyance in his eyes before he made himself settle back. It was as much with himself as with her. He'd never been the hand-holding Casanova type. Nor had he ever been put so neatly back in his place.

"No, but that was a simple statement of fact. Now, I guess I'm supposed to cross your palm with silver, but I'm fresh out."

"Palm reading's on the house." Because she was sorry she'd been so glib and abrupt, she smiled again. "When you're feeling better, I'll take you up for a tour of the haunted tower."

"I can't wait."

His dry response had her laughing. "I have a feeling about you, Max. I think you could be a lot of fun when you forget to be intense and thoughtful. Now I'm going downstairs so you can have some quiet. Be a good boy and get some more rest."

He might have been weak, but he wasn't a boy. Max rose as she did. Though the move surprised her, she gave him one of her slow, languid smiles. His color was coming back, she noted. His eyes were clear and, because he was only an inch or so taller than she, nearly on level with hers.

"Is there something else I can get you, Max?"

He felt steadier and took a moment to be grateful. "Just an answer. Are you involved with anyone?"

Her brow lifted as she swept her hair over her shoulder. "In what way?"

"It's a simple question, Lilah, and deserves a simple answer."

The lecturing quality of his tone had her frowning at him. "If you mean am I emotionally or sexually involved with a man, the answer is no. At the moment."

"Good." The vague irritation in her eyes pleased him. He'd wanted a response, and he'd gotten one.

"Look, Professor, I pulled you out of the drink. You strike me as being too intelligent a man to fall for that gratitude transference."

This time he smiled. "Transference to what?"

"Lust seems appropriate."

"You're right. I know the difference — especially when I'm feeling both at the same time." His own words surprised him. Maybe the near-death experience had rattled his brains. For a moment she looked as though she would swipe at him. Then abruptly, and beautifully, she laughed.

"I guess that was another simple statement of fact. You're an interesting man, Max."

And, she told herself as she carried the tray inside, harmless.

She hoped.

# Chapter Three

Even after he'd arranged to have funds wired from his account in Ithaca, the Calhouns wouldn't consider Max's suggestion that he move to a hotel. In truth, he didn't put up much of a fight. He'd never been pampered before, or fussed over. More, he'd never been made to feel part of a big, boisterous family. They took him in with a casual kind of hospitality that was both irresistible and gracious.

He was coming to know them and appreciate them for their varied personalities and family unity. It was a house where something always seemed to be happening and where everyone always had something to say. For someone who had grown up an only child, in a home where his bookishness had been considered a flaw, it was a revelation to be among people who celebrated their own, and each other's, interests.

C.C. was an auto mechanic who talked about engine blocks and carried the mysterious glow of a new bride. Amanda, brisk and organized, held the assistant manager's position at a nearby hotel. Suzanna ran a gardening business and devoted herself to her children. No one mentioned their father. Coco ran the house, cooked lavish meals and appreciated male company. She'd only made Max nervous when she'd threatened to read his tea leaves.

Then there was Lilah. He discovered she worked as a naturalist at Acadia National Park. She liked long naps, classical music and her aunt's elaborate desserts. When the mood struck her, she could sit, sprawled in a chair, prodding little details of his life from him. Or she could curl up in a sunbeam like a cat, blocking him and everything else around her out of her thoughts while she drifted into one of her private daydreams. Then she would stretch and smile and let them all in again.

She remained a mystery to him, a combination of smoldering sensuality and untouched innocence — of staggering openness and unreachable solitude.

Within three days, his strength had returned and his stay at The Towers was open-ended. He knew the sensible thing to do was leave, use his funds to purchase a one-way ticket back to New York and see if he could pick up a few summer tutoring jobs.

But he didn't feel sensible.

It was his first vacation and, however he had been thrust into it, he wanted to enjoy it. He liked waking up in the morning to the sound of the sea and the smell of it. It relieved him that his accident hadn't caused him to fear or dislike the water. There was something incredibly relaxing about standing on the terrace, looking across indigo or emerald water and seeing the distant clumps of islands.

And if his shoulder still troubled him from time to time, he could sit out and let the afternoon sun bake the ache away. There was time for books. An hour, even two, sitting in the shade gobbling up a novel or biography from the Calhoun library.

His life had been full of timetables, never timelessness. Here, in The Towers, with its whispers of the past, momentum of the present and hope for the future, he could indulge in it.

Underneath the simple pleasure of having no schedule to meet, no demands to answer, was his growing fascination with Lilah.

She glided in and out of the house. Leaving in the morning, she was neat and tidy in her park service uniform, her fabulous hair wound in a neat braid. Drifting home later, she would change into one of her flowing skirts or a pair of sexy shorts. She smiled at him, spoke to him, and kept a friendly but tangible distance.

He contented himself with scribbling in a notebook or entertaining Suzanna's two children, Alex and Jenny, who were already showing signs of summer boredom. He could walk in the gardens or along the cliffs, keep Coco company in the kitchen or watch the workmen in the west wing.

The wonder of it was, he could do as he chose.

He sat on the lawn, Alex and Jenny hunched on either side of him like eager frogs. The sun was a hazy silver disk behind a sheet of clouds. Playful and brisk, the breeze carried the scent of lavender and rosemary from a nearby rockery. There were butterflies dancing in the grass, easily eluding Fred's pursuits. Nearby a bird trilled insistently from the branch of a wind-gnarled oak.

Max was spinning a tale of a young boy caught up in the terrors and excitement of the revolutionary war. In weaving fact with fiction, he was keeping the children entertained and indulging in his love of storytelling.

"I bet he killed whole packs of dirty redcoats," Alex said gleefully. At six, he had a vivid and violent imagination.

"Packs of them," Jenny agreed. She was a year younger than her brother and only too glad to keep pace. "Single-handed."

"The Revolution wasn't all guns and bayonets, you know." It amused Max to see the young mouths pout at the lack of mayhem. "A lot of battles were won through intrigue and espionage."

Alex struggled with the words a moment then brightened. "Spies?"

"Spies," Max agreed, and ruffled the boy's dark hair. Because he had experienced the lack himself, he recognized Alex's hunger for a male bond.

Using a teenage boy as the catalyst, he took them through Patrick Henry's stirring speeches, Samuel Adams's courageous Sons of Liberty, through the politics and purpose of a rebellious young country to the Boston Tea Party.

Then as he had the young hero heaving chests of tea into the shallow water of Boston Harbor, Max saw Lilah drifting across the lawn.

She moved with languid ease over the grass, a graceful gypsy with her filmy chiffon skirt teased by the wind. Her hair was loose, tumbling free over the thin straps of a pale green blouse. Her feet were bare, her arms adorned with dozens of slim bracelets.

Fred raced over to greet her, leaped and yipped and made her laugh. As she bent to pet him, one of the straps slid down her arm. Then the dog bounded off, tripping himself up, to continue his fruitless chase of butterflies.

She straightened, lazily pushing the strap back into place as she continued across the grass. He caught her scent — wild and free — before she spoke.

"Is this a private party?"

"Max is telling a story," Jenny told her, and tugged on her aunt's skirt.

"A story?" The array of colored beads in her ears danced as she lowered to the grass. "I like stories."

"Tell Lilah, too." Jenny shifted closer to her aunt and began to play with her bracelets.

"Yes." There was laughter in her voice, an answering humor in her eyes as they met Max's. "Tell Lilah, too."

She knew exactly what effect she had on

a man, he thought. Exactly. "Ah . . . where was I?"

"Jim had black cork all over his face and was tossing the cursed tea into the harbor," Alex reminded him. "Nobody got shot yet."

"Right." As much for his own defense against Lilah as for the children, Max put himself back on the frigate with the fictional Jim. He could feel the chill of the air and the heat of excitement. With a natural skill he considered a basic part of teaching, he drew out the suspense, deftly coloring his characters, describing an historical event in a way that had Lilah studying him with a new interest and respect.

Though it ended with the rebels outwitting the British, without firing a shot, even the bloodthirsty Alex wasn't disappointed.

"They won!" He jumped up and gave a war hoot. "I'm a Son of Liberty and you're a dirty redcoat," he told his sister.

"Uh-uh." She sprang to her feet.

"No taxation without restoration," Alex bellowed, and went flying for the house with Jenny hot on his heels and Fred lumbering after them both.

"Close enough," Max murmured.

"Pretty crafty, Professor." Lilah leaned back on her elbows to watch him through half-closed eyes. "Making history entertaining."

"It is," he told her. "It's not just dates and names, it's people."

"The way you tell it. But when I was in school you were supposed to know what happened in 1066 in the same way you were supposed to memorize the multiplication tables." Lazily she rubbed a bare foot over her calf. "I still can't remember the twelves, or what happened in 1066 — unless that was when Hannibal took those elephants across the Alps."

He grinned at her. "Not exactly."

"There, you see?" She stretched, long and limber as a cat. Her head drifted back, her hair spreading over the summer grass. Her shoulders rolled so that the wayward strap slipped down again. The pleasure of the small indulgence showed on her face. "And I think I usually fell asleep by the time we got to the Continental Congress."

When he realized he was holding his breath, he released it slowly. "I've been thinking about doing some tutoring."

Her eyes slitted open. "You can take the boy out of the classroom," she murmured, then arched a brow. "So, what do you know about flora and fauna?"

"Enough to know a rabbit from a petunia."

Delighted, she sat up again to lean toward him. "That's very good, Professor. If the mood strikes, maybe we can exchange expertise."

"Maybe."

He looked so cute, she thought, sitting on the sunny grass in borrowed jeans and T-shirt, his hair falling over his forehead. He'd been getting some sun, so that the pallor was replaced by the beginnings of a tan. The ease she felt convinced her that she'd been foolish to be unsteady around him before. He was just a nice man, a bit befuddled by circumstances, who'd aroused her sympathies and her curiosity. To prove it, she laid a hand on the side of his face.

Max saw the amusement in her eyes, the little private joke that curved her lips before she touched them to his in a light, friendly kiss. As if satisfied with the result, she smiled, leaned back and started to speak. He circled a hand around her wrist.

"I'm not half-dead this time, Lilah."

Surprise came first. He saw it register then fade into a careless acceptance. Damn it, he thought as he slid a hand behind her

73

neck. She was so certain there would be nothing. With a combination of wounded pride and fluttery panic, he pressed his lips to hers.

She enjoyed kissing — the affection of it, the elemental physical enjoyment. And she liked him. Because of it, she leaned into the kiss, expecting a nice tingle, a comforting warmth. But she hadn't expected the jolt.

The kiss bounced through her system, starting with her lips, zipping to her stomach, vibrating into her fingertips. His mouth was very firm, very serious — and very smooth. The texture of it had a quiet sound of pleasure escaping, like a child might make after a first taste of chocolate. Before the first sensation could be fully absorbed, others were drifting through to tangle and mix.

Flowers and hot sun. The scent of soap and sweat. Smooth, damp lips and the light scrape of teeth. Her own sigh, a mere shifting of air, and the firm press of his fingers on the sensitive nape of her neck. There was something more than simple pleasure here, she realized. Something sweeter and far less tangible.

Enchanted, she lifted her hand from the carpet of grass to skim it through his hair.

He was reexperiencing the sensation of

drowning, of being pulled under by something strong and dangerous. This time he had no urge to fight. Fascinated, he slid his tongue over hers, tasting those secret flavors. Rich and dark and seductive, they mirrored her scent, the scent that had already insinuated itself into his system so that he thought he would taste that as well, each time he took a breath.

He felt something shift inside him, stretch and grow and heat until it gripped him hard by the throat.

She was outrageously sexual, unabashedly erotic, and more frightening than any woman he had known. Again he had the image of a mermaid sitting on a rock, combing her hair and luring helplessly seduced men to destruction with the promise of overwhelming pleasures.

The instinct for survival kicked in, so that he drew back. Lilah stayed as she was, eyes closed, lips parted. It wasn't until that moment that he realized he still held her wrist and that her pulse was scrambling under his fingers.

Slowly, holding on to that drugging weightlessness a moment longer, she opened her eyes. She skimmed her tongue over her lips to capture the clinging flavor of his. Then she smiled.

"Well, Dr. Quartermain, it seems history's not the only thing you're good at. How about another lesson?" Wanting more, she leaned forward, but Max scrambled up. The ground, he discovered, was as unsteady as the deck of a ship.

"I think one's enough for today."

Curious, she swung her hair back to look up at him. "Why?"

"Because . . ." Because if he kissed her again, he'd have to touch her. And if he touched her — and he desperately wanted to touch her — he would have to make love with her, there on the sunny lawn in full sight of the house. "Because I don't want to take advantage of you."

"Advantage of me?" Touched and amused, she smiled. "That's very sweet."

"I'd appreciate it if you wouldn't make me sound like a fool," he said tightly.

"Was I?" The smile turned thoughtful. "Being a sweet man doesn't make you a fool, Max. It's just that most men I know would be more than happy to take advantage. Tell you what, before you take offense at that, why don't we go inside? I'll show you Bianca's tower."

He'd already taken offense and was about to say so when her last words struck a chord. "Bianca's tower?"

"Yes. I'd like to show you." She lifted a hand, waiting.

He was frowning at her, struggling to fit the name "Bianca" into place. Then with a shake of his head, he helped her to her feet. "Fine. Let's go."

He'd already explored some of the house, the maze of rooms, some empty, some crowded with furniture and boxes. From the outside, the house was part fortress, part manor, with sparkling windows, graceful porches married to jutting turrets and parapets. Inside, it was a rambling labyrinth of shadowed hallways, sun-washed rooms, scarred floors and gleaming banisters. It had already captivated him.

She took him up a set of circular stairs to a door at the top of the east wing.

"Give it a shove, will you, Max?" she asked, and he was forced to thud the wood hard with his good shoulder. "I keep meaning to ask Sloan to fix this." Taking his hand, she walked inside.

It was a large, circular room, ringed with curving windows. A light layer of dust lay softly on the floor, but someone had tossed a few colorful pillows onto the window seat. An old floor lamp with a stained and tassled shade stood nearby.

"I imagine she had lovely things up here once," Lilah began. "To keep her company. She used to come up here to be alone, to think."

"Who?"

"Bianca. My great-grandmother. Come look at the view." Feeling a need to share it with him, she drew him to the window. From there it was all water and rock. It should have seemed lonely, Max thought. Instead it was exhilarating and heart-breaking all at once. When he put a hand to the glass, Lilah glanced over in surprise. She had done the same countless times, as if wishing for something just out of reach.

"It's . . . sad." He'd meant to say beau-tiful or breathtaking, and frowned.

"Yes. But sometimes it's comforting, too. I always feel close to Bianca in here."

*Bianca.* The name was like an insistent buzz in his head.

"Has Aunt Coco told you the story yet?"

"No. Is there a story?"

"Of course." She gave him a curious look. "I just wondered if she'd given you the Calhoun version rather than what's in the press."

A faint throbbing began in his temple where the wound was healing. "I don't know either version."

After a moment, she continued. "Bianca threw herself through this window on one of the last nights of summer in 1913. But her spirit stayed behind."

"Why did she kill herself?"

"Well, it's a long story." Lilah settled on the window seat, her chin comfortably propped on her knees, and told him.

Max listened to the tale of an unhappy wife, trapped in a loveless marriage during the heady years before the Great War. Bianca had married Fergus Calhoun, a wealthy financier, and had borne him three children. While summering on Mount Desert Island, she had met a young artist. From an old date book the Calhouns had unearthed, they knew his name had been Christian, but nothing more. The rest was legend, that had been passed down to the children from their nanny who had been Bianca's confidante.

The young artist and the unhappy wife had fallen in love, deeply. Torn between duty and her heart, Bianca had agonized over her choice and had ultimately decided to leave her husband. She had taken a few personal items, known now as Bianca's treasure, and had hidden them away in preparation. Among them had been an emerald necklace, given to her on the birth of her first son and second child, Lilah's grandfather. But rather than going to her lover, Bianca had thrown herself through the tower window. The emeralds have never been found.

"We didn't know the story until a few months ago," Lilah added. "Though I'd seen the emeralds."

His mind was whirling. Nagged by the pain, he pressed his fingers to his temple. "You've seen them?"

She smiled. "I dreamed about them. Then during a séance —"

"A séance," he said weakly, and sat.

"That's right." She laughed and patted his hand. "We were having a séance, and C.C. had a vision." He made a strangled sound in his throat that had her laughing again. "You had to be there, Max. Anyway, C.C. saw the necklace, and that's when Aunt Coco decided it was time to pass on the Calhoun legend. To get where we are today, Trent fell in love with C.C. and decided not to buy The Towers. We were in pretty bad shape and were on the point of being forced to sell. He came up with the idea of turning the west wing into a hotel, with the St. James's name. You know the St. James hotels?"

Trenton St. James, Max thought. Lilah's

brother-in-law owned one of the biggest hotel corporations in the country. "By reputation."

"Well, Trent hired Sloan to handle the renovations — and Sloan fell for Amanda. All in all, it couldn't have worked out better. We were able to keep the house, combine it with business, and culled two romances out of the bargain."

Annoyance flickered into her eyes, darkening them. "The downside has been that the story about the necklace leaked, and we've been plagued with hopeful treasure hunters and out-and-out thieves. Just a few weeks ago, some creep nearly killed Amanda and stole stacks of the papers we'd been sorting through to try to find a clue to the necklace."

"Papers," he repeated as a sickness welled in his stomach. It was coming back now and with such force he felt as though he were being battered on the rocks again. Calhoun, emeralds, Bianca.

"What's wrong, Max?" Concerned, Lilah leaned over to lay a hand on his brow. "You're white as a sheet. You've been up too long," she decided. "Let me take you down so you can rest."

"No, I'm fine. It's nothing." He jerked away to rise and pace the room. How was he going to tell her? How could he tell her, after she had saved his life, taken care of him? After he'd kissed her? The Calhouns had opened their home to him, without hesitation, without question. They had trusted him. How could he tell Lilah that he had, however inadvertently, been working with men who were planning to steal from her?

Yet he had to. Marrow-deep honesty wouldn't permit anything else.

"Lilah . . ." He turned back to see her watching him, a combination of concern and wariness in her eyes. "The boat. I re-member the boat."

Relief had her smiling. "That's good. I thought it would come back to you if you stopped worrying. Why don't you sit down, Max? It's easier on the brain."

"No." The refusal was sharp as he con-centrated on her face. "The boat — the man who hired me. His name was Caufield. Ellis Caufield."

She spread her hands. "And?"

"The name doesn't mean anything?"

"No, should it?"

Maybe he was wrong, Max thought. Maybe he was letting her family story meld in his mind with his own experience. "He's about six foot, very trim. About forty. Dark-blond hair graying at the temples."

"Okay."

Max let out a frustrated breath. "He contacted me at Cornell about a month ago and offered me a job. He wanted me to sort through, catalogue and research some family papers. I'd get a generous salary, and several weeks on a yacht — plus all my expenses and time to work on my book."

"So, seeing as you're not brain damaged, you took the job."

"Yes, but damn it, Lilah, the papers — the receipts, the letters, the ledgers. They had your name on them."

"Mine?"

"Calhoun." He jammed his useless hands into his pockets. "Don't you understand? I was hired, and worked on that boat for a week, researching your family history from the papers that were stolen from you."

She only stared. It seemed a long time to Max before she unfolded herself from the window seat and stood. "You're telling me that you've been working for the man who tried to kill my sister?"

"Yes."

She never took her eyes from his. He

could almost feel her trying to get into his thoughts, but when she spoke, her voice was very cool. "Why are you telling me this now?"

Frazzled, he dragged a hand through his hair. "I didn't remember it all until now, until you told me about the emeralds."

"That's odd, isn't it?"

He watched the shutter come down over her eyes and nodded. "I don't expect you to believe me, but I didn't remember. And when I took the job, I didn't know."

She continued to watch him carefully, measuring every word, every gesture, every expression. "You know, it seemed strange to me that you hadn't heard about the necklace, or the robbery. It's been in the press for weeks. You'd have to be living in a cave not to have heard."

"Or a classroom," he murmured. Caufield's mocking words about having more intelligence than wit came back to him and made him wince. "Look, I'll tell you whatever I can before I leave."

"Leave?"

"I can't imagine any of you will want me to stay after this."

She considered him, instinct warring against common sense. With a long sigh, she lifted a hand. "I think you'd better tell the whole story to the whole family, all at once. Then we'll decide what to do about it."

It was Max's first family meeting. He hadn't grown up in a democracy, but under his father's uncompromising dictatorship. The Calhouns did things different. They gathered around the big mahogany dining room table, so completely united that Max felt like an intruder for the first time since he'd awakened upstairs. They listened, occasionally asking questions as he repeated what he had told Lilah in the tower.

"You didn't check his references?" Trent asked. "You just contracted to do a job with a man you'd never met, and knew nothing about?"

"There didn't seem to be any reason to. I'm not a businessman," he said wearily. "I'm a teacher."

"Then you won't object if we check yours." This from Sloan.

Max met the suspicious eyes levelly. "No."

"I already have," Amanda put in. Her fingers were tapping against the wood of the table as all eyes turned to her. "It

85

seemed the logical step, so I made a couple of calls."

"Leave it to Mandy," Lilah muttered. "I guess it never occurred to you to discuss it with the rest of us."

"No."

"Girls," Coco said from the head of the table. "Don't start."

"I think Amanda should have talked about this." The Calhoun temper edged Lilah's voice. "It concerns all of us. Besides, what business does she have poking into Max's life?"

They began to argue heatedly, all four sisters tossing in opinions and objections. Sloan kicked back to let it run its course. Trent closed his eyes. Max merely stared. They were discussing him. Didn't they realize they were arguing about him, tossing him back and forth across the table like a Ping-Pong ball?

"Excuse me," he began, and was totally ignored. He tried again and earned his first smile from Sloan. "Damn it, knock it off!" It was his annoyed professor's voice and did the trick. All of the women stopped to turn on him with irritated eyes.

"Look, buster," C.C. began, but he cut her off.

"You look. In the first place, why would I

86

be telling you everything if I had some ulterior motive? And since you want to corroborate who I am and what I do, why don't you stop pecking at each other long enough to find out?"

"Because we like to peck at each other," Lilah told him grandly. "And we don't like anyone getting in the way while we're at it."

"That'll do." Coco took advantage of the lull. "Since Amanda's already checked on Max — though it was a bit impolite —"

"Sensible," Amanda objected.

"Rude," Lilah corrected.

They might have been off and running again, but Suzanna held up a hand. "Whatever it was, it's done. I think we should hear what Amanda found out."

"As I was saying." Amanda flicked a glance over at Lilah. "I made a couple of calls. The dean of Cornell speaks very highly of Max. As I recall the terms were 'brilliant' and 'dedicated.' He's considered one of the foremost experts on American history in the country. He graduated magna cum laude at twenty, and had his doctorate by twenty-five."

"Egghead," Lilah said with a comforting smile when Max shifted in his seat.

"Our Dr. Quartermain," Amanda continued, "comes from Indiana, is single and has no criminal record. He's been on the staff at Cornell for over eight years, and has published several well-received articles. His most recent was an overview of the social-political atmosphere in America prior to World War I. In academic circles, he's considered a wunderkind, serious minded, unflaggingly responsible, with unlimited potential." Sensing his embarrassment, Amanda softened her tone. "I'm sorry for intruding, Max, but I didn't want to take any chances, not with my family."

"We're all sorry." Suzanna smiled at him. "We've had an unsettling couple of months."

"I understand that." And they certainly couldn't know how much he detested the term *wunderkind*. "If my academic profile eases your minds, that's fine."

"There's one more thing," Suzanna continued. "None of this explains what you were doing in the water the night Lilah found you."

Max gathered his thoughts while they waited. It was easy to take himself back now, as easy as it was for him to put himself into the Battle of Bull Run or Woodrow Wilson's White House.

"I'd been working on the papers. A storm was coming in so the sea was rough. I guess I'm not much of a sailor. I was trying to crawl out on deck, for some air, when I heard Caufield talking to Captain Hawkins."

As concisely as he could, he told them what he had heard, how he had realized what he'd gotten into.

"I don't know what I was going to do. I had some wild idea about getting the papers and getting off the boat so I could take them to the police. Not very brilliant considering the circumstances. In any case, they caught me. Caufield had a gun, but this time the storm was on my side. I got up on deck, and took my chances in the water."

"You jumped overboard, in the middle of a storm?" Lilah asked.

"It wasn't very smart."

"It was very brave," she corrected.

"Not when you consider he was shooting at me." Frowning, Max rubbed a hand over the bandage on his temple.

"The way you describe this Ellis Caufield doesn't fit." Amanda tapped her fingers again as she thought it through. "Livingston, the man who stole the papers was dark haired, only about thirty."

"So, he dyed his hair." Lilah lifted her hands. "He couldn't come back using the same name and the same appearance. The police have his description."

"I hope you're right." A slow, humorless smile spread over Sloan's face. "I hope the sonofabitch is back so I can have another go at him."

"So we all can have another go at him," C.C. corrected. "The question is, what do we do now?"

They began to argue about that, with Trent telling his wife she wasn't going to do anything — Amanda reminding him it was a Calhoun problem — Sloan suggesting hotly that she keep out of it. Coco decided it was time for brandy and was ignored.

"He thinks I'm dead," Max murmured, almost to himself. "So he feels safe. He's probably still close by, on the same boat. The *Windrider.*"

"You remember the boat?" Lilah held up a hand, signaling for silence. "You can describe it?"

"In detail," Max told her with a small smile. "It was my first yacht."

"So we take that information to the police." Trent glanced around the table, then nodded. "And we do a little checking ourselves. The ladies know the island as well as they know this house. If he's on it, or around it, we'll find him."

"I'm looking forward to it." Sloan glanced over at Max and went with his instincts. "You in, Quartermain?"

Surprised, Max blinked, then found himself smiling. "Yeah, I'm in."

*I went to Christian's cottage. Perhaps it was risky as I might have been seen by some acquaintance, but I wanted so badly to see where he lived, how he lived, what small things he kept around him.*

*It's a small place near the water, a square wooden cottage with its rooms crowded with his paintings and smelling of turpentine. Above the kitchen is a sun-drenched loft for his studio. It seemed to me like a doll's house with its pretty windows and low ceilings — old leafy trees shading the front and a narrow porch dancing along the back where we could sit and watch the water.*

*Christian says that at low tide the water level drops so that you can walk across the smooth rocks to the little glade of trees beyond. And at night, the air is full of sound. Musical crickets, the hoot of owls, the lap of temperate water.*

*I felt at home there, as quietly content as I have been in my life. It seemed to me that we had lived there together for years. When I told Christian, he gathered me close, just to hold me.*

*"I love you, Bianca," he said. "I wanted you to come here. I needed to see you in my house, watch you stand among my things." When he drew me away, he was smiling. "Now, I'll always see you here, and I'll never be without you."*

*I wanted to swear to him I would stay. God, the words leaped into my throat only to be blocked there by duty. Wretched duty. He must have sensed it for he kissed me then, as if to seal the words inside.*

*I had only an hour with him. We both knew I would have to go back to my husband, to my children, to the life I had chosen before I met him. I felt his arms around me, tasted his lips, sensed the straining need inside him that was such a vibrant echo of my own.*

*"I want you." I heard my own whisper and felt no shame. "Touch me, Christian. Let me belong to you." My heart was racing as I pressed wantonly against him. "Make love to me. Take me to your bed."*

*How tightly his arms gripped me, so*

*tightly I couldn't get my breath. Then his hands were on my face, and I felt the tremor in his fingertips. His eyes were nearly black. So much could be read there. Passion, love, desperation, regret.*

*"Do you know how often I've dreamed of it? How many nights I've lain awake aching for you?" Then he released me to stride across the room to where my portrait hung on his wall. "I want you, Bianca, every time I take a breath. And I love you too much to take what can't be mine."*

*"Christian —"*

*"Do you think I could let you go if I'd ever touched you?" There was anger now, ripe and violent as he whirled back. "I hate knowing that we sneak like sinners just to spend an hour together, as innocent as children. If I don't have the strength to turn away from you completely, then I will have enough to keep you from taking a step you'd only regret."*

*"How could I regret belonging to you?"*

*"Because you already belong to someone else. And every time you go back to him, I dream of killing him with my bare hands if only because he can look at you when I can't. If we took this last step, I'd leave you no choice. There would be no*

going back to him, Bianca. No going back to your home, or your life."

And I knew it was true, as he stood between me and the image of me he'd created.

So I left him to come home, to tie a ribbon in Colleen's hair, to chase a ball with Ethan, to dry Sean's tears when he scraped his knee. To dine in miserable politeness with a husband who is more and more of a stranger to me.

Christian's words were true, and it is a truth I must face. The time is coming when I will no longer be able to live in both worlds, but must choose one, only one.

# Chapter Four

"I have the most marvelous idea," Coco announced. Like a ship in full sail, she streamed into the kitchen where Lilah, Max, Suzanna and her family were having breakfast.

"Good for you," Lilah said over a bowl of chocolate-chip ice cream. "Anyone who can think at this hour deserves a medal, or should be committed."

Like a mother hen, Coco checked the herbs she had potted on the window. She clucked over the basil before she turned back. "I have no idea why I didn't think of it before. It's really so —"

"Alex is kicking me under the table."

"Alex, don't kick your sister," Suzanna said mildly. "Jenny, don't interrupt."

"I wasn't kicking her." Milk dribbled down Alex's chin. "She got her knee in the way of my foot."

"Did not."

"Did too."

"Turkey face."

"Booger head."

"Alex." Suzanna bit down on the inside of her lip to maintain the properly severe maternal disapproval. "Do you want to eat that cereal or wear it?"

"She started it," he muttered.

"Did not," Jenny said under her breath.

"Did too."

Another glance at their mother had them subsiding to eye each other with grim dislike over their cereal bowls.

"Now that that's settled." Amused, Lilah licked her spoon. "What's your marvelous idea, Aunt Coco?"

"Well." She fluffed her hair, absently checking her reflection in the toaster, approving it, then beaming. "It all has to do with Max. Really it's so obvious. But, of course, we were worried about his health, then it's so difficult to think clearly with this construction going on. Do you know one of those young men was out on the terrace this morning in nothing but a pair of jeans and a tool belt? Very distracting." She peeked out of the kitchen window, just in case.

"I'm sorry I missed it." Lilah winked at Max. "Was it the guy with the long blond hair tied back with a leather thong?"

"No, the one with dark curly hair and a

mustache. I must say, he's extremely well built. I suppose one would keep fit swinging hammers or whatever all day. The noise is a bother, though. I hope it doesn't disturb you, Max."

"No." He'd learned to flow with Coco's rambling thought patterns. "Would you like some coffee?"

"Oh, that's sweet of you. I believe I will." She sat while he got up to pour her a cup. "They've literally transformed the billiard room already. Of course, we've a long way to go — thank you, dear," she added when Max set a cup of coffee in front of her. "And all those tarps and tools and lumber make things unsightly. But it will all be worth it in the end." As she spoke, she doctored her coffee with cream and heaps of sugar. "Now, where was I?"

"A marvelous idea," Suzanna reminded her, putting a restraining hand on Alex's shoulder before he could fling any soggy cereal at his sister.

"Oh, yes." Coco set her cup down without taking a sip. "It came to me last night when I was doing the tarot cards. There were some personal matters I'd wanted to resolve, and I'd wanted to get a feel for this other business."

"What other business?" Alex wanted to know.

"Grown-up business." Lilah dug a knuckle into his ribs to make him laugh. "Boring."

"You guys better go find Fred." Suzanna checked her watch. "If you want to go with me today, you've got five minutes."

They were up and shooting out of the room like little bullets. Surreptitiously Max rubbed his shin where Alex's foot had connected.

"The cards, Aunt Coco?" Lilah said when the explosion was over.

"Yes. I learned that there was danger, past and future. Disconcerting." She cast a worried look over both her nieces. "But we're to have help dealing with it. There seemed to be two different sources of aid. One was cerebral, the other physical — potentially violent." Uneasy, she frowned a little. "I couldn't place the physical source, though it seemed I should because it was from someone familiar. I thought it might be from Sloan. He's so, well, Western. But it wasn't. I'm quite sure it wasn't." Brushing that aside, she smiled again. "But naturally the cerebral source is Max."

"Naturally." Lilah patted his hand as he

shifted uncomfortably in his chair. "Our resident genius."

"Don't tease him." Suzanna rose to take bowls to the sink.

"Oh, he knows I don't just like him for his brain. Don't you, Max?"

He was mortally afraid he would blush in a minute. "If you keep interrupting your aunt, you'll be late for work."

"And so will I," Suzanna pointed out. "What's the idea, Aunt Coco?"

She'd started to drink again, and again set the coffee down untouched. "That Max should do what he came here to do." Smiling, she spread her manicured hands. "Research the Calhouns. Find out as much as possible about Bianca, Fergus, everyone involved. Not for that awful Mr. Caufield or whatever his name is, but for us."

Intrigued, Lilah thought the idea over. "We've already been through the papers."

"Not with Max's objective, and scholarly eye," Coco pointed out. Already fond of him, she patted his shoulder. Her interpretation of the cards also had indicated that he and Lilah would suit very well. "I'm sure if he put his mind to it, he could come up with all kinds of wonderful theories."

"It's a good idea." Suzanna came back to the table. "How do you feel about it?"

Max considered. Though he didn't put any stock in tarot cards, he didn't want to hurt Coco's feelings. Besides, however she had come up with the idea, it was sound. It would be a way of paying them back and a way to justify staying on in Bar Harbor a few more weeks.

"I'd like to do something. There's a good chance that even with the information I gave them the police won't find Caufield. While everyone's looking for him, I could be concentrating on Bianca and the necklace."

"There." Coco sat back. "I knew it."

"I'd wanted to check out the library, the newspaper, interview some of the older residents, but Caufield shut down the idea." The more he thought about it, the more Max liked the notion of working on his own. "Claimed he wanted everything to come out of the family papers, or his own sources." He moved his cup aside. "Obviously he couldn't give me a free hand or I'd find out the truth."

"Now you have a free hand," Lilah put in. It amused her that she could already see the wheels turning. "But I don't think you'll find the necklace in a library."

"But I may find a photograph of it, or a description."

Lilah simply smiled. "I've already given you that."

He didn't put much stock in dreams and visions, either, and shrugged. "All the same, I might find something tangible. And I'll certainly find something on Fergus and Bianca Calhoun."

"I suppose it'll keep you busy." Unoffended by his lack of faith in her mystical beliefs, Lilah rose. "You'll need a car to get around. Why don't you drop me off at work and use mine?"

Irked by her lack of faith in his research abilities, Max spent hours in the library. As always, he felt at home there, among stacks of books, in the center of the murmuring quiet, with a notebook at his elbow. To him, research was a quest — perhaps not as exciting as riding a white charger. It was a mystery to be solved, though the clues were less adventurous than a smoking gun or a trail of blood.

But with patience, cleverness and skill, he was a knight, or a detective, carefully working his way to an answer.

The fact that he had always been drawn to such places had disappointed his father bitterly, Max knew. Even as a boy he had preferred mental exercise over the physical.

He had not picked up the torch to follow his father's blaze of glory on the high school football field. Nor had he added trophies to the shelf.

Lack of interest and a long klutzy adolescence had made him a failure in sports. He had detested hunting, and on the last outing his father had pressured him into had come up with a vicious asthma attack rather than a buck.

Even now, years later, he could remember his father's disgusted voice creeping into his hospital room.

"Damn boy's a pansy. Can't understand it. He'd rather read than eat. Every time I try to make a man out of him, he ends up wheezing like an old woman."

He'd gotten over the asthma, Max reminded himself. He'd even made something out of himself, though his father wouldn't consider it a man. And if he never felt completely adequate, at least he could feel competent.

Shrugging off the mood, he went back to his quest.

He did indeed find Fergus and Bianca. There were little gems of information peppered through the research books. In the familiar comfort of a library, Max took reams of notes and felt the excitement build.

He learned that Fergus Calhoun had been self-made, an Irish immigrant who through grit and shrewdness had become a man of wealth and influence. He'd landed in New York in 1888, young, poor and, like so many who had poured into Ellis Island, looking for his fortune. Within fifteen years, he had built an empire. And he had enjoyed flaunting it.

Perhaps to bury the impoverished youth he had been, he had surrounded himself with the opulent, muscling his way into society with wealth and will. It was in polite, exclusive society that he had met Bianca Muldoon, a young debutante of an old, established family with more gentility than money. He had built The Towers, determined to outdo the other vacationing rich, and had married Bianca the following year.

His golden touch had continued. His empire had grown, and so had his family with the birth of three children. Even the scandal of his wife's suicide in the summer of 1913 hadn't affected his monetary fortune.

Though he had become somewhat of a recluse after her death, he had continued to wield his power from The Towers. His daughter had never married and, estranged from her father, had gone to live in Paris.

His youngest son had fled, after a peccadillo with a married woman, to the West Indies. Ethan, his eldest child, had married and had two children of his own, Judson, Lilah's father, and Cordelia Calhoun, now Coco McPike.

Ethan had died in a sailing accident, and Fergus had lived out the last years of his long life in an asylum, committed there by his family after several outbursts of violent and erratic behavior.

An interesting story, Max mused, but most of the details could have been gleaned from the Calhouns themselves. He wanted something else, some small tidbit that would lead him in another direction.

He found it in a tattered and dusty volume titled *Summering in Bar Harbor*.

It was such a flighty and poorly written work that he nearly set it aside. The teacher in him had him reading on, as he would read a student's ill-prepared term paper. It deserved a C- at best, Max thought. Never in his life had he seen so many superlatives and cluttered adjectives on one page. Glamorously to gloriously, magnificent to miraculous. The author had been a wide-eyed admirer of the rich and famous, someone who saw them as royalty. Sumptuous, spectacular and splendiferous.

The syntax made Max wince, but he plodded on.

There were two entire pages devoted to a ball given at The Towers in 1912. Max's weary brain perked up. The author had certainly attended, for the descriptions were in painstaking detail, from fashion to cuisine. Bianca Calhoun had worn gold silk, a flowing sheath with a beaded skirt. The color had set off the highlights in her titian hair. The scooped bodice had framed . . . the emeralds.

They were described in glowing and exacting detail. Once the adjectives and the romantic imagery were edited, Max could see them. Scribbling notes, he turned the page. And stared.

It was an old photograph, perhaps culled from a newspaper print. It was fuzzy and blurred, but he had no trouble recognizing Fergus. The man was as rigid and stern-faced as the portrait the Calhouns kept over the mantel in the parlor. But it was the woman sitting in front of him that stopped Max's breath.

Despite the flaws of the photo, she was exquisite, ethereally beautiful, timelessly lovely. And she was the image of Lilah. The porcelain skin, the slender neck left bare with a mass of hair swept up in the

Gibson style. Oversize eyes he was certain would have been green. There was no smile in them, though her lips were curved.

Was it just the romance of the face, he wondered, or did he really see some sadness there?

She sat in an elegant lady's chair, her husband behind her, his hand on the back of the chair rather than on her shoulder. Still, it seemed to Max that there was a certain possessiveness in the stance. They were in formal wear — Fergus starched and pressed, Bianca draped and fragile. The stilted pose was captioned, Mr. and Mrs. Fergus Calhoun, 1912.

Around Bianca's neck, defying time, were the Calhoun emeralds.

The necklace was exactly as Lilah had described to him, the two glittering tiers, the lush single teardrop that dripped like emerald water. Bianca wore it with a coolness that turned its opulence into elegance and only intensified the power.

Max trailed a fingertip along each tier, almost certain he would feel the smoothness of the gems. He understood why such stones become legends, to haunt men's imaginations and fire their greed.

But it eluded him, a picture only. Hardly

realizing what he was doing, he traced Bianca's face and thought of the woman who had inherited it. '

There were women who haunt and inflame.

Lilah paused in her stroll down the nature path to give her latest group time to photograph and rest. They had had an excellent crowd in the park that day, with a hefty percentage of them interested enough to hike the trails and be guided by a naturalist. Lilah had been on her feet for the best part of eight hours, and had covered the same ground eight times — sixteen if she counted the return trip.

But she wasn't tired, yet. Nor did her lecture come strictly out of a guidebook.

"Many of the plants found on the island are typically northern," she began. "A few are subarctic, remaining since the retreat of the glaciers ten thousand years ago. More recent specimens were brought by Europeans within the last two hundred and fifty years."

With a patience that was a primary part of her, Lilah answered questions, distracted some of the younger crowd from trampling the wildflowers and fed information on the local flora to those who were interested. She identified the beach pea, the seaside goldenrod, the late-blooming harebell. It was her last group of the day, but she gave them as much time and attention as the first.

In any case she always enjoyed this seaside stroll, listening to the murmur of pebbles drifting in the surf or the echoing call of gulls, discovering for herself and the tourists what treasures lurked in the tide pools.

The breeze was light and balmy, carrying that ancient and mysterious scent that was the sea. Here the rocks were smooth and flat, worn to elegance by the patient ebb and flow of water. She could see the glitter of quartz running in long white rivers down the black stone. Overhead, the sky was a hard summer blue, nearly cloudless. Under it, boats glided, buoys clanged, orange markers bobbed.

She thought of the yacht, the *Windrider*, and though she searched as she had on each tour, she saw nothing but sleek tourist boats or the sturdy crafts of lobstermen.

When she saw Max hiking the nature trail down to join the group, she smiled. He was on time, of course. She'd expected no less. She felt a slow tingle of warmth when his gaze lifted from his feet to her face. He really had wonderful eyes, she thought. Intent and serious, and just a little shy.

As always when she saw him, she had an urge to tease him and an underlying longing to touch. An interesting combination, she thought now, and one she couldn't remember experiencing with anyone else.

She looked so cool, he thought, the mannish uniform over the willowy feminine form. The military khaki and the dangle of gold and crystal at her ears. He wondered if she knew how suited she was to stand before the sea while it bubbled and swayed at her back.

"At the intertidal zone," she began, "life has acclimated to tidal change. In spring, we have the highest and lowest tides, with a rise and fall of 14.5 feet."

She went on in that easy, soothing voice, talking of intertidal creatures, survival and food chains. Even as she spoke, a gull glided to perch on a nearby rock to study the tourists with a beady, expectant eye. Cameras clicked. Lilah crouched down beside a tide pool. Fascinated by her description of life there, Max moved to see for himself.

There were long purple fans she called

dulse, and she had the children in the group groaning when she told them it could be eaten raw or boiled. In the dark little pool of water, she found a wealth of living things, all waiting, she said, for the tide to come in again before they went back to business.

With a graceful fingertip she pointed out the sea anemones that looked more like flowers than animals, and the tiny slugs that preyed on them. The pretty shells that were mollusks and snails and whelks. She sounded like a marine biologist one moment and a stand-up comedian the next.

Her appreciative audience bombarded her with questions. Max caught one teenage boy staring at her with a moony kind of lust and felt instant sympathy.

Tossing her braid behind her back, she wound up the tour, explaining about the information available at the visitors center, and the other naturalist tours. Some of the group started to meander their way back along the path, while others lingered behind to take more pictures. The teenager loitered behind his parents, asking any question his dazzled brain could form on the tide pools, the wildflowers and, though he wouldn't have looked twice at a robin, the birds. When he'd exhausted all angles, and his mother called impatiently for the second time, he trudged reluctantly off.

"This is one nature walk he won't forget any time soon," Max commented.

She only smiled. "I like to think they'll all remember some pieces of it. Glad you could make it, Professor." She did what her instincts demanded and kissed him fully, softly on the mouth.

Looking back, the teenager experienced a flash of miserable envy. Max was simply knocked flat. Lilah's lips were still curved as she eased away.

"So," she asked him, "how was your day?"

Could a woman kiss like that then expect him to continue a normal conversation? Obviously this one could, he decided and took a long breath. "Interesting."

"Those are the best kind." She began to walk up the path that would lead back to the visitors center. Arching a brow, she glanced over her shoulder. "Coming?"

"Yeah." With his hands in his pockets, he started after her. "You're very good."

Her laugh was light and warm. "Why, thank you."

"I meant — I was talking about your job."

"Of course you were." Companionably

she tucked an arm through his. "It's too bad you missed the first twenty minutes of the last tour. We saw two slate-colored juncos, a double-crested cormorant and an osprey."

"It's always been one of my ambitions to see a slate-colored junco," he said, and made her laugh again. "Do you always do the same trail?"

"No, I move around. One of my favorites is Jordan Pond, or I might take a shift at the Nature Center, or hike up in the mountains."

"I guess that keeps it from getting boring."

"It's never boring, or I wouldn't last a day. Even on the same trail you see different things all the time. Look." She pointed to a thatch of plants with narrow leaves and faded pink blooms. "Rhodora," she told him. "A common azalea. A few weeks ago it was at peak. Stunning. Now the blooms will die off, and wait until spring." She brushed her fingertips over the leaves. "I like cycles. They're reassuring."

Though she claimed to be an unenergetic woman, she walked effortlessly along the trail, keeping an eye out for anything of interest. It might be lichen clinging to a rock, a sparrow in flight or a spray of hawk-weed. She liked the scent here, the sea they were leaving behind, the green smell of trees that began to crowd in to block the view.

"I didn't realize that your job kept you on your feet most of the day."

"Which is why I prefer to stay off them at all other times." She tilted her head to look at him. "Tell you what though, the next time I have an afternoon, I'll give you a more in-depth tour. We can kill two birds with one stone, so to speak. Take in the scenery, and poke around for your friend, Caufield."

"I want you to stay out of it."

The statement took her so off guard that she walked another five feet before it registered. "You what?"

"I want you to stay out of it," he repeated. "I've been giving it a lot of thought."

"Have you?" If he had known her better, he might have recognized the hint of temper in the lazy tone. "And just how did you come to that particular conclusion?"

"He's dangerous." The voice, laced with hints of fanaticism came back clearly. "I think he might even be unbalanced. It's certain that he's violent. He's already shot at your sister, and at me. I don't want you getting in his way."

"It's not a matter of what you want. It's family business."

"It's been mine since I took a swim in a storm." Caught between sunlight and shade on the path, he stopped to put his hands on her shoulders. "You didn't hear him that night, Lilah. I did. He said nothing would stop him from getting the necklace, and he meant it. This is a job for the police, not for a bunch of women who —"

"A bunch of women who what?" she interrupted with a gleam in her eyes.

"Who are too emotionally involved to react cautiously."

"I see." She nodded slowly. "So it's up to you and Sloan and Trent, the big, brave men to protect us poor, defenseless women and save the day?"

It occurred, a bit too late, that he was on very shaky ground. "I didn't say you were defenseless."

"You implied it. Let me tell you something, Professor, there isn't one of the Calhoun women who can't handle herself and any man who comes swaggering down the road. That includes geniuses and unbalanced jewel thieves."

"There, you see?" His hands lifted from

her shoulders, then settled again. "Your re-action is pure emotion without any logic or thought."

The heated eyes narrowed. "Do you want to see emotion?"

Besides brains, he prided himself on a certain amount of street smarts. Cautious, he eased back. "I don't think so."

"Fine. Then I suggest you take care with your phrasing, and think twice before you tell me to keep out of something that is wholly my concern." She brushed by him to continue toward the voices around the visitors center.

"Damn it, I don't want you hurt."

"I don't intend to get hurt. I have a very low threshold for pain. But I'm not going to sit around with my hands folded while someone plots to steal what's mine."

"The police —"

"Haven't been a hell of a lot of help," she snapped. "Did you know that Interpol has been looking for Livingston, and his many aliases, for fifteen years? No one was able to trace him after he shot at Amanda and stole our papers. If Caufield and Livingston are one in the same, then it's up to us to protect what's ours."

"Even if it means getting your brains bashed in?"

She tossed a look over her shoulder. "I'll worry about my brains, Professor. You worry about yours."

"I'm not a genius," he muttered, and surprised a smile out of her.

The exasperation on his face took the edge off her temper. She stepped off the path. "I appreciate the concern, Max, but it's misplaced. Why don't you wait out here, sit on the wall? I've got to go in and get my things."

She left him muttering to himself. He only wanted to protect her. Was that so wrong? He cared about her. After all, she had saved his life. Scowling, he sat on the stone wall. People were milling in and out of the building. Children were whining as parents tugged, dragged or carried them to cars. Couples were strolling along hand in hand while others pored eagerly through guide books. He saw a lot of skin broiled Maine-lobster-red by the sun.

He glanced at his own forearms and was surprised to see that they were tanned. Things were changing, he realized. He was getting a tan. He had no schedule to keep, no itinerary to follow. He was involved in a mystery, and with an incredibly sexy woman.

"Well . . ." Lilah adjusted the strap of

her purse on her arm. "You're looking very smug."

He looked up at her and smiled. "Am I?"

"As a cat with feathers in his mouth. Want to let me in on it?"

"Okay. Come here." He rose, gave her one firm yank and closed his mouth over hers. All of his new and amazed feelings poured into the kiss. If he took the kiss deeper than expected, it only added to the dawning pleasure of discovery. If kissing her made the people walking around them disappear, it only accented the newness. Starting fresh.

It was happiness rather than lust she felt from him. It confused her. Or perhaps it was the way his lips slid over hers that dimmed coherent thought. She didn't resist. The reason for her earlier irritation was already forgotten. All she knew now was that it felt wonderful, somehow perfect, to be standing with him on the sunny patio, feeling his heart thud against hers.

As his mouth slipped from hers, she let out a long, pleased sigh, opening her eyes slowly. He was grinning at her, and the delighted expression on his face had her smiling back. Because she wasn't sure what to do with the tender feelings he tugged from her, she patted his cheek.

"Not that I'm complaining," she began. "But what was that for?"

"I just felt like it."

"An excellent first step."

Laughing, he swung an arm around her shoulder as they started toward the parking lot. "You've got the sexiest mouth I've ever tasted."

He didn't see the cloud come into her eyes. If he had, she couldn't have explained it. It always came down to sex, she supposed and made an effort to shrug the vague disappointment away. Men usually saw her just that way, and there was no reason to let it start bothering her now, particularly when she'd enjoyed the moment as much as he.

"Glad I could oblige," she said lightly. "Why don't you drive?"

"All right, but first I've got something to show you." After settling into the driver's seat, he picked up a manilla envelope. "I went through a lot of books in the library. There are several mentions of your family in histories and biographies. There was one in particular I thought would interest you."

"Hmm." She was already stretched out and thinking of a nap.

"I made a copy of it. It's a picture of Bianca."

"A picture?" She straightened again. "Really? Fergus destroyed all her pictures after she died, so I've never seen her."

"Yes, you have." He drew the copy out and handed it to her. "Every time you look in the mirror."

She said nothing, but with her eyes focused on the grainy copy she lifted a hand to her own face. The same jaw, the same mouth, nose, eyes. Was this why she felt the bond so strongly? she wondered, and felt tears burn her throat.

"She was beautiful," Max said quietly.

"So young." The words came out as a sigh. "Younger than I when she died. She'd already fallen in love when this was taken. You can see it, in her eyes."

"She's wearing the emeralds."

"Yes, I know." As he had, she traced a fingertip over them. "How difficult it must have been for her, tied to one man, loving another. And the necklace — a symbol of one man's hold on her, and a reminder of her children."

"Is that how you see it, a symbol?"

"Yes. I think her feelings for it, about it, were terribly strong. Otherwise, she wouldn't have hidden it." She slipped the paper back into the envelope. "A good day's work, Professor."

"It's just a beginning."

As she looked at him, she linked her fingers with his. "I like beginnings. Everything that follows has such possibilities. We'll go home and show this to everyone, after we make a couple of stops."

"Stops?"

"It's time for another beginning. You need some new clothes."

He hated shopping. He told her, repeatedly and firmly, but she blithely ignored him and strolled from shop to shop. He held his ground on a fluorescent T-shirt, but lost it again over one depicting a lobster dressed like a maître d'.

She wasn't intimidated by clerks, but sailed through the process of selection and purchase with a languid air of pure relaxation. Most of the merchants called her by name, and during the chats that accompanied the buying and selling, she would casually ask about a man fitting Caufield's description.

"Are we finished yet?" There was a plea in his voice that made her chuckle as they stepped out onto the sidewalk again. It was teeming with people in bright summer clothes.

"Not quite." She turned to study him.

Harassed, definitely. Adorable, absolutely. His arms were full of bags and his hair was falling into his eyes. Lilah brushed it back. "How are you fixed for underwear?"

"Well, I . . ."

"Come on, there's a shop right down here that has great stuff. Tiger prints, obscene sayings, little red hearts."

"No." He stopped dead. "Not on your life."

It was a struggle, but she kept her composure. "You're right. Completely unsuitable. We'll just stick with those nice white briefs that come three to a package."

"For a woman with no brothers, you sure know a lot about men's underwear." He shifted the bags, and as an afterthought, shoved half of them into her arms. "But I think I can handle this one on my own."

"Okay. I'll window-shop."

She was easily diverted by a window filled with crystals of different sizes and shapes. They dangled from wire, shooting colored light behind the glass. Beneath them was a display of handmade jewelry. She was on the point of stepping inside to wrangle over a pair of earrings when someone bumped her from behind.

"Sorry." The apology was terse. Lilah

glanced up at a burly man with a weathered face and graying hair. He looked a great deal more irritated than the slight bump warranted, and something about the pale eyes had her taking a step back. Still, she shrugged and smiled.

"It's all right."

Frowning after him a moment, she started to turn back into the shop. She spotted Max a few feet away, staring in shock. Then he was moving fast, and the expression on his face had her catching her breath.

"Max —"

With one hard shove, he had her in the shop. "What did he say to you?" he demanded with an edge to his voice that had her eyes widening. "Did he touch you? If the bastard put his hands on you —"

"Hold on." Since they had most of the people in the shop staring, Lilah kept her voice low. "Calm down, Max. I don't know what you're talking about."

There was a violence trembling through his blood he'd never experienced before. The echo of it in his eyes had several tourists edging back out the door. "I saw him standing next to you."

"That man?" Baffled, she glanced out the window, but he had long since moved on. "He just bumped into me. The sidewalks are crowded in the summer."

"He didn't say anything to you?" He didn't even realize that his hands had firmed into fists and that the fists were ready to do damage. "He didn't hurt you?"

"No, of course not. Come on, let's go sit down." Her tone was soothing now as she nudged him out. But instead of taking one of the benches that lined the street, Max kept Lilah behind him and searched the crowd. "If I'd known buying underwear would put you in such a state, Max, I wouldn't have brought it up."

There was fury in his eyes when he whirled around. "It was Hawkins," he said grimly. "They're still here."

# Chapter Five

She didn't know what to make of him. Alone, with the lamplight glowing gold, Lilah sat in the tower room, watching night fall gently over water and rock. And thought of Max. He wasn't nearly as simple a man as she had believed at first — and as she was certain he believed of himself.

One moment he was shy and sweet and easily intimidated. The next he was as fierce as a Viking, the mild blue eyes electric, the poet's mouth grim. The metamorphosis was as fascinating as it was baffling, and left Lilah off balance. It wasn't a sensation she cared for.

After he had seen the man he called Hawkins, Max had all but dragged her to the car — muttering under his breath all the way — bundled her inside, then had driven off. Her idea about following Hawkins had been briskly and violently vetoed. Back at The Towers, he'd called the police, relating the information as calmly as he would list assigned reading for a student. Then, in a typical male move had powwowed with Sloan and Trent.

The authorities had not yet located Caufield's boat, nor, from Max's descriptions, had they identified either Caufield or Hawkins.

It was much too complicated, Lilah decided. Thieves and aliases and international police. She preferred the simple. Not the humdrum, she thought, but the simple. Life had been anything but since the press had begun their love affair with the Calhoun emeralds, and things had become only more convoluted since Max had washed up on the beach.

But she was glad he had. She wasn't sure why. Certainly she'd never considered the shy and brainy sort her type. It was true that she enjoyed men in general, simply for being men. An offshoot, she supposed, from living in a female household most of her life. But when she dated, she most often looked for fun and easy companionship. Someone to dance with or to laugh with over a meal. She'd always hoped she would fall in love with one of those carefree, uncomplicated men and start a carefree, uncomplicated life.

Sober college professors with outdated

notions of chivalry and serious minds hardly met the qualifications.

Yet he was so sweet, she thought with a little smile. And when he kissed her, there was nothing sober or cerebral about it.

With a little sigh, she wondered just what she should do about Dr. Maxwell Quartermain.

"Hey." C.C. poked her head through the doorway. "I thought I'd find you in here."

"Then I must be becoming too predictable." Happy to have company, Lilah curled up her legs to make room on the window seat. "What's going on with you, Mrs. St. James?"

"Nearly finished the reconditioning on that Mustang." She sighed as she sat. "Lord, what a honey. I had an electrical system that gave me fits today, and two tune-ups." An unaccustomed fatigue was dragging at her, making her close her eyes and think about an early night. "Then all this excitement at home. Imagine, you bumping into one of the characters the cops are after."

"The curse and blessing of small towns."

"I cruised around a little before I came home." C.C. rolled her tired shoulders. "Down to Hulls Cove and back."

"You shouldn't be poking around alone."

"Just looking." C.C. shrugged. "Anyway, I didn't see anything. Our fearless men are out right now on search and destroy."

A quick bolt of alarm shot into Lilah. "Max went with them?"

On a yawn, C.C. opened her eyes. "Sure. Suddenly, they're the Three Musketeers. Is there anything more annoying than machismo?"

"Tooth decay," Lilah said absently, but there were nerves bumping along in her system she didn't care for. "I thought Max was going to stick to the research books."

"Well, he's one of the boys now." She patted Lilah's ankle. "Don't worry, honey. They can handle themselves."

"For heaven's sake, he's a history professor. What if they actually run into trouble?"

"He already has," C.C. reminded her. "He's tougher than he looks."

"What makes you think so?" Unreasonably distressed, Lilah got up to pace. The unaccustomed show of energy had C.C. lifting a brow.

"The man jumped out of a boat in the middle of a storm and almost made it to shore, despite the fact he'd been grazed by a bullet. The next day, he was on his feet again — looking like hell, but on his feet.

127

There's a stubborn streak behind those quiet eyes. I like him."

Restless, Lilah moved her shoulders. "Who doesn't? He's a likable man."

"Well, with everything that Amanda found out — the wonder boy stuff — you'd expect him to be conceited, or stiff-necked. But he's not. He's sweet. Aunt Coco's ready to adopt him."

"He is sweet," Lilah agreed as she sat again. "And I don't want him to get hurt because of some misguided sense of gratitude."

C.C. leaned forward to look into her sister's eyes. There was more than casual concern in them, she thought, and smiled to herself. "Lilah, I know you're the mystic in the family, but I'm getting definite vibes. Are you getting serious about Max?"

"Serious?" The word had Lilah's nerves stretching. "Of course not. I'm fond of him, and I feel a certain responsibility toward him." And when he kisses me, I go directly to meltdown. She frowned a little. "I enjoy him," she slowly added.

"He's very attractive."

"You're a married woman now, kiddo."

"But not blind. There's something appealing about all that intelligence, those romantic and scholarly looks." She waited a beat. "Don't you think?"

Lilah sat back. Her lips were curved again to match the amusement in her eyes. "Are you apprenticing with Aunt Coco as matchmaker?"

"Just checking. I guess I'm so happy I want everyone I love to feel the same way."

"I am happy." She took a long, limbering stretch. "I'm too lazy not to be."

"Speaking of lazy, I feel like I could sleep for a week. Since Trent's out playing Hardy Boys, I think I'll go to bed." C.C. started to rise when a wave of dizziness had her plopping down again. Lilah was up like a shot and bending over her.

"Hey. Hey, honey. Are you all right?"

"Got up too fast, that's all." As the light grayed, she lifted a hand to her spinning head. "I feel a little . . ."

Moving fast, Lilah shoved C.C.'s head between her knees. "Just breathe slow. Take it easy."

"This is stupid." But she did as she was told until the faintness passed. "I'm just overtired. Maybe I'm coming down with something, damn it."

"Mmm." Because she suspected just what C.C. had come down with, Lilah's lips curved. "Tired? Have you been feeling sick?"

"Not really." Steadier, C.C. straightened.

"Out of sorts, I guess. A little queasy the past couple of mornings, that's all."

"Honey." With a laugh, Lilah tapped her knuckles on her sister's head. "Wake up and smell the baby powder."

"Huh?"

"Hasn't it occurred to you that you could be pregnant?"

"Pregnant?" The dark green eyes widened like saucers. "Pregnant? Me? But we've only been married a little over a month."

Lilah laughed again and cupped C.C.'s face in her hands. "You haven't spent all that time playing pinochle, have you?"

C.C.'s mouth opened and closed before she managed to form a word. "It just never crossed my mind. . . . A baby." Her eyes changed, misting, softening. "Oh, Lilah."

"Could be Trenton St. James IV."

"A baby," C.C. repeated, and laid a hand over her stomach in a gesture that was filled with awe and protectiveness. "Do you really think?"

"I really think." She slid back on the seat to hug C.C. tight. "I don't have to ask you how you feel about it. It's all over your face."

"Don't say anything to anyone yet. I want to be sure." Laughing, she squeezed

Lilah against her. "Suddenly I don't feel tired at all. I'll call the doctor first thing in the morning. Or maybe I should pick up one of those tests from the drugstore. I could do both."

Lilah let her ramble. Long after C.C. had gone, the echoes of her joy remained in the room.

It was what the tower needed, Lilah thought. That jolt of pure happiness. She stayed where she was, content now, watching the moon rise. Half-full, bone white, it hung in the sky and had her dreaming.

What would it be like, being with someone, smugly married, having a child growing inside you? Making a life with someone who would know you so well. Know every part of you and love you despite the flaws. Maybe because of them.

Lovely, she thought. It would be simply lovely. And if she had yet to find that for herself, she had only to look at C.C. and Amanda to know it could happen.

With some regret she switched off the light and started downstairs to her room. The house was quiet now. She imagined it must be at least midnight, and everyone had gone to bed. A wise choice, she mused, but she couldn't seem to shake the restlessness.

To comfort herself, she indulged in a long, fragrant bath before slipping into her favorite robe. Those were the little things that always pleased her — hot, scented water, cool, thin silk. Still unsettled, she walked out onto the terrace to see if the night air would lull her.

It was much too romantic, she thought. The glitter of moonlight silvering the trees, the quiet whoosh of water on rock, the scents from the garden. As she stood, a bird, as restless as she, began a lonely night song. It made her long for something. For someone. A touch, a whisper in the dark. An arm around her shoulders.

A mate.

Not just the physical, but the emotional, the spiritual partner. She had had men desire her and knew that could never be enough. There had to be someone who could look beyond the color of her hair or the shape of her face and into her heart.

Perhaps she was asking for too much, Lilah thought with a sigh. But wasn't that better than asking for too little? In the meantime she would have to concentrate on other things and leave her heart in fate's capricious hands.

She had started to turn back into her room when a movement caught her eye. In the swaying moonlight she saw two shadows bent low, moving with silent swiftness across the lawn. Before she could do more than register the shapes, they had melted into the garden.

She didn't even think about it. A home was meant to be defended. Her bare feet were noiseless on the stone steps as she walked down them. Whoever was trespassing on Calhoun territory was about to get the scare of their lives.

Like a ghost, she slipped into the garden, the robe floating around her. There were voices, muffled and excited, a faint yellow beam of a flashlight. There was a laugh, quickly smothered, then the sound of a shovel striking earth.

That more than anything brought the Calhoun temper bubbling to the surface. With the courage of the righteous, she strode forward.

"What the hell do you think you're doing?"

The shovel clanged on stone as it was dropped. The flashlight went spiraling into the azaleas. Two teenagers, wound up with the treasure hunt, looked around wildly for the source of the voice. They saw the pale figure of a woman draped in white. Summing up her quarry, Lilah lifted her arms for effect, knowing the full sleeves would billow nicely.

"I am guardian of the emeralds." She nearly chuckled, pleased with the way her voice floated. "Do you dare to face the curse of the Calhouns? Hideous death is certain for any who defile this ground. Run, if you value your lives."

They didn't have to be told twice. The treasure map they had paid ten bucks for fluttered to the ground as they raced back down the path, shoving each other and tripping over their own scrambling feet. Chuckling to herself, Lilah picked up the map.

She'd seen its like before. Some enterprising soul was making them up and selling them to gullible tourists. After shoving it into her pocket, she decided to give her two uninvited guests a little extra boost. She dashed after them. Ready to send up a ghostly wail, she burst out of the garden.

The wail turned into a grunt as she rammed into another shadow. Stopped in a dead run, Max overbalanced, swore, then went tumbling to the ground on top of her.

"What the hell are you doing?"

"It's me," she managed, then sucked in a breath. "What the hell are you doing?"

"I saw someone. Stay here."

"No." She grabbed his arms and held on. "It was just a couple of kids with a treasure map. I scared them off."

"You —" Furious, he braced on an elbow. Despite the dark, the anger shone clearly in his eyes. "Are you out of your mind?" he demanded. "You came out here, alone, to face down two intruders?"

"Two terrified teenagers with a treasure map," she corrected. Her chin lifted. "It's my house."

"I don't give a damn whose house it is. It might have been Caufield and Hawkins. It might have been anyone. No one with an ounce of sense follows potential robbers into a dark garden alone, in the middle of the night."

She had her breath back and studied him blandly. "What were you doing?"

"I was going after them," he began, then caught her expression. "That's different."

"Why? Because I'm a woman?"

"No. Well, yes."

"That's stupid, untrue and sexist."

"That's sensible, factual and sexist." They'd been arguing in furious whispers. Now he sighed. "Lilah, you might have been hurt."

"The only one who hurt me was you, with that flying tackle."

"I didn't tackle you," he muttered. "I was watching them and didn't see you. And I certainly didn't expect to find you out here sneaking around in the dark."

"I wasn't sneaking." She blew hair out of her eyes. "I was playing ghost, and very effectively."

"Playing ghost." He shut his eyes. "Now I know you're out of your mind."

"It worked," she reminded him.

"That's beside the point."

"It's precisely the point, the other being that you knocked me down before I could finish the job."

"I've already apologized."

"No, you haven't."

"All right. I'm sorry if I . . ." He started to push himself off her and made the mistake of glancing down. Her robe had come loose during the fall and lay open to the waist. Like alabaster, her breasts glowed in the moonlight. "Oh, Lord," he managed to say through suddenly dry lips.

She'd lost her breath again. Lying still, she watched his eyes change. Irritation to shock, shock to wonder, wonder to a deep and dark desire. As his gaze skimmed up, came back to hers, every muscle in her body melted like hot wax.

No one had ever looked at her just that

way. There was such intensity in his eyes, the same focused concentration they had held when he'd struggled to block out pain. They roamed to her mouth, lingering there until her lips trembled apart on his name.

It was like moving into a dream, he thought as he lowered himself onto her again. Everything was just one click out of focus, soft and fuzzy. His hands were in her hair, lost in it. Beneath his, her lips were warm, beautifully warm. Her arms came around him as if they had been waiting. He heard her sigh, long and deep.

His mouth was so gentle on hers, as if he were afraid she might vanish if he dared too much too soon. Yet she could feel the tension in the way he held himself, the way his hands fisted in her hair, the way his breath shuddered out as he brushed his lips over hers.

Her limbs grew heavy, her head light. Though she wanted to keep her eyes open, as his were, they drifted closed. The most pleasant of aches coursed through her as he nibbled delicately at her parted lips. Her murmur mixed with his, indecipherable.

The grass whispered as she shifted beneath him. Its cool, fresh fragrance seemed perfectly suited to him. As his fingers slid softly over her breast, she heard her own quiet moan of acceptance.

She was unbelievably perfect, he thought dizzily. Like some fantasy conjured on a lonely night. Long slender limbs, silky skin, an avid and generous mouth. The sheer physical pleasure of her was like a drug, and he was already addicted.

Murmuring her name, he skimmed his lips to her throat. There her pulse beat like thunder, heating her skin so that her scent tangled with each breath he took. Tasting her was like dining on sin. Touching her was paradise. He brought his lips back to hers to lose himself on that glorious edge between heaven and hell.

She could almost feel herself floating an inch above the cool grass. Her body felt free as air, soft as water. When his mouth met hers again, she let herself drift into the new kiss. Then it happened.

It was not the sweet click of a door opening that she had been hoping for. It was a rushing roar, like a gust of wind sweeping through her body. Behind it, speeding in its wake, was a pain, sharp, sweet and stunning. She stiffened against it, her cry of protest muffled against his lips.

If she had slapped him, his passion wouldn't have cooled more quickly. He jerked back to see her staring at him, her eyes wide and filled with fear and confusion. Appalled by his behavior, he scrambled to his knees. He was trembling, he realized, So was she. Small wonder. He had acted like a maniac, knocking her down, pawing her.

Lord help him, he wanted to do it again.

"Lilah . . ." His voice was a husky rasp, and he struggled to clear it. She didn't move a muscle. Her eyes never left his. He wanted to stroke her cheek, to gather her close and hold her, but was afraid to touch her again. "I'm sorry. Very sorry. You looked so beautiful. I guess I lost my head."

She waited for a moment, for the balance and ease that was so much a part of her. But it didn't come. "Is that it?"

"I . . ." What did she want him to say? he wondered. He felt like a monster already. "You're an incredibly desirable woman," he said carefully. "But that's no excuse for what happened just now."

What had happened? She was afraid she had fallen in love with him, and if she had, love hurt. She didn't like it one damn bit. "You want me, physically."

He cleared his throat. *Want* wasn't the word. *Craved* was closer, but still fell pitifully short of the mark. As gently as he would for a child, he brought her robe together again. "Any man would," he said, nerves straining.

Any man, she thought and closed her eyes on the slash of disappointment. She hadn't been waiting for any man, but for one man. "It's all right, Max." Her voice was a shade overbright as she sat up. "No harm done. It's just a matter of us finding the other physically attractive. Happens all the time."

"Yes, but —" Not to him, he thought. Not like this. He frowned down at a blade of grass. It was easier for her, he supposed. She was so open, so uninhibited. There had probably been dozens of men in her life. Dozens, he thought on a jolt of fury that had him tearing the blade in two. "What do you suggest we do about it?"

"Do about it?" Her smile was strained, but he wasn't even looking at her. "Why don't we just see if it passes. Like the flu."

He looked at her then, with something dangerous edging his eyes. "It won't. Not for me. I want you. A woman like you would know just how badly I want you."

The words brought both a thrill and an

ache. "A woman like me," she repeated softly. "Yes, that's the crux of it, isn't it, Professor?"

"The crux of what?" he began, but she was already on her feet.

"A woman who enjoys men, and who's very generous with them."

"I didn't mean —"

"One who'll wrestle half-naked on the grass. A little bohemian for you, Dr. Quartermain, but you're not above experimenting a little bit here and there — with a woman like me."

"Lilah, for God's sake —" He too was on his feet, baffled.

"I wouldn't apologize again if I were you. There's certainly no need." Hurt beyond measure, she tossed back her hair. "Not when it concerns a woman like me. After all, you've got me pegged, don't you?"

Good Lord, were those tears in her eyes? He gestured helplessly. "I haven't got a clue."

"Right again. All you understand about this is your own wants." She swallowed the tears. "Well, Professor, I'll take them under consideration and let you know."

Completely lost, he watched her gather the skirts of her robe and dart up the

141

stairs. Moments later her terrace doors closed with an audible click.

She didn't cry. Lilah reminded herself it was an exhausting experience that usually left her with a miserable headache. She couldn't think of a single man who was worth the trouble. Instead, she dragged open the drawer of her nightstand and pulled out her emergency bar of chocolate.

After plopping down onto the bed, she took a healthy bite and stared at the ceiling.

Sexy. Beautiful. Desirable. Big damn deal, she thought and bit off another hunk. For all his celebrated brains, Maxwell Quartermain was as big a jerk as any other man. All he saw was a pretty package, and once he'd unwrapped it, that would be that. He wouldn't see any substance, any of the softer needs.

Oh, he was more polite than most. A gentleman to the last, she thought in disgust. She hadn't had to untangle herself. God knew he'd been in a hurry to do that for himself.

Lost his head. At least he was honest, she thought, and brushed impatiently at a tear that sneaked past her guard.

She knew the kind of image she projected. It rarely bothered her what people thought of her. She understood herself, was comfortable with Lilah Maeve Calhoun. There certainly was no shame in the fact that she enjoyed men. Though she hadn't enjoyed them to the extent that others, including, she supposed, her family might think.

Uninhibited? Perhaps, but that wasn't synonymous with promiscuity. Did she flirt? Yes, it came naturally to her, but it wasn't done with malice or guile.

If a man flirted with women he was suave. If a woman flirted, she was a tease. Well, as far as she was concerned the game between the sexes was a two-way street, and she enjoyed playing. And as for the good professor . . .

She curled up into a tight, defensive ball. Oh, God, he'd hurt her. All that stuttering, apologizing, explaining. And all the time he looked so appalled.

*A woman like you.* The phrase played back in her head.

Couldn't he see what he'd done to her with that careful tenderness? Hadn't he been able to feel how deeply he'd affected her? All she had wanted was for him to touch her again, to smile in that sweet, shy way of his and tell her that he cared. About who she was, what she was, how she felt inside. She'd wanted comfort and reassurance, and he'd given her excuses. She had looked up at him, with the stab of love still streaking through her, the terror of it still trembling, and he'd jerked back as if she'd clipped him on the jaw.

She wished she had. If this was love, she didn't want her share after all.

Because it was quiet, or perhaps because her ears were tuned for him, she heard Max come up the steps, sensed him hesitate near her doors. She stopped breathing, though her heart picked up a quick beat. Would he come in now, push those doors open and come to her, tell her what she wanted so badly to hear? She could almost see his hand reach for the knob. Then she heard his footsteps again as he moved on down the terrace to his own room.

Her breath came out in a sigh. It wouldn't fit his principles to enter her bedroom uninvited. Outside, on the grass, he'd been following his instincts rather than his intellect, she admitted. No one was more in favor of that than Lilah. For him, it had been the moment, the moon, the mood. It was difficult to blame him, certainly impossible to expect him to feel as she felt. Want as she wanted.

She sincerely hoped he didn't sleep a wink.

She sniffled, swallowed chocolate, then began to think. Only two months before, C.C. had come to her, hurt and infuriated because Trent had kissed her, then apologized for it.

Pursing her lips, Lilah rolled onto her back again. Maybe it was typical male stupidity. It was difficult to fault the breed for something they were born with. If Trent had apologized because he'd cared about her sister, then it could follow that Max had played the same cards.

It was an interesting theory, and one that shouldn't be too difficult to prove. Or disprove, she thought with a sigh. Either way, it was probably best to know before she got in any deeper. All she needed was a plan.

Lilah decided to do what she did best, and slept on it.

# Chapter Six

It wasn't difficult in a house the size of The Towers to avoid someone for a day or two. Max noted that Lilah had effortlessly stayed out of his way for that amount of time. He couldn't blame her, not after how badly he had botched things.

Still, it irked him that she wouldn't accept a simple and sincere apology. Instead she'd turned it into . . . damned if he knew what she'd turned it into. The only thing he was sure of was that she'd twisted his words, and their meaning, then had stalked off in a snit.

And he missed her like crazy.

He kept busy enough, buried in his research books, poring over the old family papers that Amanda had meticulously filed according to date and content. He found what he considered the last public sighting of the necklace in a newspaper feature covering a dinner dance in Bar Harbor, August 10, 1913. Two weeks before Bianca's death.

Though he considered it a long shot, he began a list of every servant's name he came across who had worked at The Towers the summer of 1913. Some of them could conceivably be alive. Tracking them or their families down would be difficult but not impossible. He had interviewed the elderly before on their memories of their youth. Quite often, those memories were as clear as crystal.

The idea of talking to someone who had known Bianca, who had seen her — and the necklace — excited him. A servant would remember The Towers as it had been, would have knowledge of their employers' habits. And, he had no doubt, would know their secrets.

Confident in the notion, Max bent over his lists.

"Hard at work, I see."

He glanced up, blinking, to see Lilah in the doorway of the storeroom. She didn't have to be told she'd dragged him out of the past. The blank, owlish look he gave her made her want to hug him. Instead she leaned lazily against the jamb.

"Am I interrupting?"

"Yes — no." Damn it, his mouth was watering. "I was just, ah, making a list."

"I have a sister with the same problem."

147

She was wearing a full-skirted sundress in sheer white cotton, her gypsy hair like cables of flames against it. Long chunks of malachite swung at her ears when she crossed the room.

"Amanda." Because the pencil had gone damp in his hand, he set it aside. "She did a terrific job of cataloging all this information."

"She's a fiend for organization." Casually she rested a hip on the card table he was using. "I like your shirt."

It was the one she'd chosen for him, with the cartoon lobster. "Thanks. I thought you'd be at work."

"It's my day off." She slid off the table to round it and lean over his shoulder. "Do you ever take one?"

Though he knew it was ridiculous, he felt his muscles bunch up. "Take what?"

"A day off." Brushing her hair aside, she turned her face toward his. "To play."

She was doing it deliberately, there could be no doubt. Maybe she enjoyed watching him make a fool out of himself. "I'm busy." He managed to tear his gaze away from her mouth and stared down at the list he was making. He couldn't read a word. "Really busy," he said almost desperately. "I'm trying to note down all the names of the people who worked here the summer Bianca died."

"That's quite an undertaking." She leaned closer, delighted with his reaction to her. It had to be more than lust. A man didn't fight so hard against basic lust. "Do you want some help?"

"No, no, it's a one-man job." And he wanted her to go away before he started to whimper.

"It must have been a terrible time here, after she died. Even worse for Christian, hearing about it, reading about it, and not being able to do anything. I think he loved her very much. Have you ever been in love?"

Once again, she drew his eyes back to hers. She wasn't smiling now. There was no teasing light in her eyes. For some reason he thought it was the most serious question she had ever asked him.

"No."

"Neither have I. What do you think it's like?"

"I don't know."

"But you must have an opinion." She leaned a little closer. "A theory. A thought."

He was all but hypnotized. "It must be like having your own private world. Like a dream, where everything's intensified, a bit off balance and completely yours."

"I like that." He watched her lips curve, could almost taste them. "Would you like to take a walk, Max?"

"A walk?"

"Yes, with me. Along the cliffs."

He wasn't even sure he could stand. "A walk would be good."

Saying nothing, she offered him her hand. When he rose, she led him through the terrace doors.

The wind was up, pushing the clouds across a blue sky. It tore at Lilah's skirts and sent her hair flying. Unconcerned, she strolled into it, her hand lightly clasped in his. They crossed the lawn and left the busy sounds of building behind.

"I'm not much on hiking," she told him, "since I spend most days doing just that, but I like to go to the cliffs. There are very strong, very beautiful memories there."

He thought again of all the men who must have loved her. "Yours?"

"No, Bianca's, I think. And if you don't choose to believe in such things, the view's worth the trip."

He started down the slope beside her. It felt easy, simple, even friendly. "You're not angry with me anymore."

"Angry?" Deliberately she lifted a brow. She had no intention of making things too simple. "About what?"

"The other night. I know I upset you."

"Oh, that."

When she added nothing else, he tried again. "I've been thinking about it."

"Have you?" Her eyes, mysterious with secrets, lifted to his.

"Yes. I realize I probably didn't handle it very well."

"Would you like another chance?"

He stopped dead in his tracks and made her laugh.

"Relax, Max." She gave him a friendly kiss on the cheek. "Just give it some thought. Look, the mountain cranberry's blooming." She bent to touch a spray of pink bell-shaped flowers that clung to the rocks. Touch, but not pick, he noted. "It's a wonderful time for wildflowers up here." Straightening, she tossed her hair back. "See those?"

"The weeds?"

"Oh, and I thought you were a poet." With a shake of her head, she had her hand tucked back in his. "Lesson number one," she began.

As they walked, she pointed out tiny clumps of flowers that pushed out of crev-

151

ices or thrived in the thin, rocky soil. She showed him how to recognize the wild blueberry that would be ripe and ready the following month. There was the flutter of butterfly wings and the drone of bees deep in the grass. With her, the common became exotic.

She snipped off a thin leaf, crushing it to release a pungent fragrance that reminded him of her skin.

He stood with her on a precipice thrown out over the water. Far below, spray fumed on the rock, beating them smooth in a timeless war. She helped him spot the nests, worked cleverly onto narrow ridges and clinging tenaciously to faults in the rocks.

It was what she did every day for groups of strangers, and for herself. There was a new kind of pleasure in sharing it all with him, showing him something as simple and special as the tiny white sandwort or the wild roses that grew as tall as a man. The air was like wine, freshened by the wind, so that she sat on a huddle of rock to drink it with each breath.

"It's incredible here." He couldn't sit. There was too much to see, too much to feel.

"I know." She was enjoying his pleasure

as much as the sun on her face and the wind in her hair. It was in his as well, streaming through the shaggy locks. There was fascination in his eyes, darkening them to indigo as the faint smile curved his lips. The wound on his temple was healing, but she thought it would leave a slight scar that would add something rakish to the intelligent face.

As a thrush began to trill, she circled her knee with her arms. "You look good, Max."

Distracted, he glanced over his shoulder. She was sitting easily on the rocks, as relaxed as she would have been on a cushy sofa. "What?"

"I said you look good. Very good." She laughed as his jaw dropped. "Hasn't anyone ever told you you're attractive?"

What game was she playing now? he wondered, and shrugged uncomfortably. "Not that I remember."

"No star-struck undergraduate, no clever English Lit professor? That's very remiss. I imagine more than one of them tried to catch your eye — and a bit more than that — but you were too buried in books to notice."

His brows drew together. "I haven't been a monk."

"No." She smiled. "I'm already aware of that."

Her words reminded him vividly of what had happened between them two nights before. He had touched her, tasted her, had managed, barely, to pull himself back before taking her right there on the grass. And she had rushed off, he remembered, furious and hurt. Now she was taunting him, all but daring him to repeat the mistake.

"I never know what to expect from you."

"Thank you."

"That wasn't a compliment."

"Even better." Her eyes slanted, half-closed now against the sun. When she spoke, her voice was almost a purr. "But you like predictability, don't you, Professor? Knowing what happens next."

"Probably as much as you like irritating me."

Laughing, she held out a hand. "Sorry, Max, sometimes it's irresistible. Come on, sit down. I promise to behave."

Wary, he sat on the rock beside her. Her skirts fluttered teasingly around her legs. In a gesture he felt was almost maternal, she patted his thigh.

"Want to be pals?" she asked him.

"Pals?"

"Sure." Her eyes danced with amusement. "I like you. The serious mind, the honest soul." He shifted, making her laugh. "The way you shuffle around when you're embarrassed."

"I do not shuffle."

"The authoritative tone when you're annoyed. Now you're supposed to tell me what you like about me."

"I'm thinking."

"I should have added your dry wit."

He had to smile. "You're the most self-possessed person I've ever met." He glanced at her. "And you're kind, without making a fuss about it. You're smart, but you don't make a fuss about that, either. I guess you don't make a fuss about anything."

"Too tiring." But his words had a glow spreading around her heart. "It's safe to say we're friends then?"

"Safe enough."

"That's good." She gave his hand a gentle squeeze. "I think it's important for us to be friends before we're lovers."

He nearly fell off the rock. "Excuse me?"

"We both know we want to make love." When he began to stammer she gave him a patient smile. She'd thought it through very carefully and was sure — well, nearly sure — this was right for both of them. "Relax, it isn't a crime in this state."

"Lilah, I realize I've been . . . that is, I know I've made advances."

"Advances." Desperately in love, she laid a hand on his cheek. "Oh, Max."

"I'm not proud of my behavior," he said stiffly, and had her hand sliding away. "I don't want . . ." His tongue tied itself into knots.

The hurt was back, a combination of rejection and defeat she detested. "You don't want to go to bed with me?"

Now his stomach was in knots, as well. "Of course I do. Any man —"

"I'm not talking about any man." They were the poorest two words he could have chosen. It was him, only him she cared about. She needed to hear him say he wanted her, if nothing else. "Damn it, I'm talking about you and me, right here, right now." Temper pushed her off the rock. "I want to know about your feelings. If I wanted to know how any man felt, I'd pick up the phone or drive into the village and ask any man."

Keeping his seat, he considered her. "For someone who does most things slowly, you have a very quick temper."

"Don't use that professorial tone on me."

It was his turn to smile. "I thought you liked it."

"I changed my mind." Because her own attitude confused her, she turned away to look out over the water. It was important to remain calm, she reminded herself. She was always able to remain calm effortlessly. "I know what you think of me," she began.

"I don't see how you can, when I'm far from sure myself." He took a moment to gather his thoughts. "Lilah, you're a beautiful woman —"

She whirled back, eyes electric. "If you tell me that again, I swear, I'll hit you."

"What?" Completely baffled, he threw his hands up and rose. "Why? Good God, you're frustrating."

"That's much better. I don't want to hear that my hair's the color of sunset, or that my eyes are like sea foam. I've heard all that. I don't care about that."

He began to think that being a monk, completely divorced from the mysterious female, had its advantages. "What do you want to hear?"

"I'm not going to tell you what I want to hear. If I do, then what's the point?"

At wit's end, he raked both hands through his hair. "The point is, I don't know what the point is. One minute you're telling me about sandwarts —"

"Sandwort," she said between her teeth.

"Fine. We're talking about flowers and friendship, and the next you're asking me if I want to take you to bed. How am I supposed to react to that?"

Her eyes narrowed. "You tell me."

He went on a mental search for safe ground and found none. "Look, I realize you're used to having men . . ."

Her narrowed eyes glinted. "Having them what?"

If he was going to sink, Max decided, he might as well go down with a flourish. "Just shut up." He grabbed her arms, dragged her hard against him and crushed his mouth to hers.

She could taste the frustration, the temper, the edgy passion. It seemed that what he was feeling was a reflection of her own emotions. For the first time, she struggled against him, fighting to hold back her response. And for the first time, he ignored the protest and demanded one.

His hand was in her billowing hair, pulling her head back so that he could plunder mindlessly. Her body was arched, straining away from him, but he locked her closer, so close even the wind couldn't slip between them.

This was different, she thought. No man had ever forced her to . . . feel. She didn't want this ache, these needs, this desperation. Since the last time they had been together she had convinced herself that love could be painless, and simple and comfortable, if only she were clever enough.

But there was pain. No amount of passion or desire could completely coat it.

Furious with both of them, he tore his mouth from hers, but his hands dug into her shoulders. "Is that what you want?" he demanded. "Do you want me to forget every rule, every code of decency? You want to know how I feel? Every time I'm around you I itch to get my hands on you. And when I do I want to drag you off somewhere and make love to you until you forget that there was ever anyone else."

"Then why don't you?"

"Because I care about you, damn it. Enough to want to show you some respect. And too much to want to be just the next man in your bed."

The temper faded from her eyes to be replaced by a vulnerability more poignant than tears. "You wouldn't be." She lifted a hand to his face. "You're a first for me,

Max. There's never been anyone else like you." He said nothing, and the doubt in his eyes had her hand slipping to her side again. "You don't believe me."

"I've found it difficult to think clearly since I met you." Abruptly he realized he was still gripping her shoulders, and gentled his hold. "You could say you dazzle me."

She looked down. How close she had come, she realized, to telling him everything that was in her heart. And humiliating herself, embarrassing him. If it was just to be physical between them, then she would be strong enough to accept it. "Then we'll leave it at that for now." She managed a smile. "We've been taking ourselves too seriously anyway." To comfort herself, she gave him a soft, lingering kiss. "Friends?"

He let out a long breath. "Sure."

"Walk back with me, Max." She slipped a hand into his. "I feel like a nap."

An hour later, he sat on the sunny terrace outside of his room, the notebook on his lap forgotten and his mind crowded with thoughts of her.

He didn't come close to understanding her — was certain he couldn't come closer if he had several decades to consider the problem. But he did care, enough to add a good jolt of fear to the rest of the emotions she pulled out of him. What did he, a painfully middle-class college professor, have to offer a gorgeous, exotic and free-spirited woman who exuded sex like other women exuded perfume?

He was so pitifully inept that he was stuttering around her one minute and grabbing her like a Neanderthal the next.

Maybe the best thing for him was to remember that he was more comfortable and certainly more competent with his books than with women.

How could he tell her that he wanted her so badly he could hardly breathe? That he was terrified to act on his needs because, once done, he knew he'd never be free of her? An easy summer romance for her, a life-altering event for him.

He was falling in love with her, which was ridiculous. He couldn't have a place in her life, and hoped he was smart enough to get a grip on his emotions before they carried him too far. In a few weeks, he would go back to his nicely ordered routine. It was what he wanted. It had to be.

And he couldn't survive it if she haunted him.

"Max?" Trent, taking the circular route to the west wing, stopped. "Interrupting?"

"No." Max glanced down at the blank sheet on his lap. "Nothing to interrupt."

"You looked like you were trying to puzzle out a particularly difficult problem. Anything to do with the necklace?"

"No." Max looked up, squinted against the sun. "Women."

"Oh. Good luck." He lifted a brow. "Particularly if it's a Calhoun woman."

"Lilah." Weary, Max rubbed his hands over his face. "The more I think about her, the less I understand."

"A perfect start in a relationship." Because he was feeling smug about his own, Trent took a moment and sat down. "She's a fascinating woman."

"I've decided the word's *unstable*."

"Beautiful."

"You can't tell her that. She bites your head off." Intrigued, he studied Trent. "Does C.C. threaten to hit you if you tell her she's beautiful?"

"Not so far."

"I thought it might be a family trait." He began to tap his pencil against the pad. "I don't know very much about women."

"Well then, I should tell you all I know." Steepling his fingers, Trent sat back.

"They're frustrating, exciting, baffling, wonderful and infuriating."

Max waited a moment. "That's it?"

"Yeah." He glanced up, lifting a hand in salute as Sloan approached.

"Coffee break?" Sloan asked, and finding the idea appealing, took out a cigar.

"A discussion on women," Trent informed him. "You might like to add something to my brief dissertation."

Sloan took his time lighting the cigar. "Stubborn as mules, mean as alley cats and the best damn game in town." He blew out smoke and grinned at Max. "You've got a thing for Lilah, don't you?"

"Well, I —"

"Don't be bashful." Sloan's grin widened as he poked out with the cigar. "You're among friends."

Max wasn't accustomed to discussing women, and certainly not his feelings toward a particular woman. "It would be difficult not to be interested."

Sloan gave a hoot of laughter and winked at Trent. "Son, you'd be dead if you weren't interested. So what's the problem?"

"I don't know what to do about her."

Trent's lips curved. "Sounds familiar. What do you want to do?"

Max slanted Trent a long, slow look that had him chuckling.

"Yeah, there is that." Sloan puffed contentedly on his cigar. "Is she, ah, interested?"

Max cleared his throat. "Well, she's indicated that she — that is, earlier we took a walk up on the cliffs, and she . . . yeah."

"But?" Trent prompted.

"I'm already in over my head."

"Then you might as well go under for the third time," Sloan told him, and eyed the tip of his cigar. " 'Course, if you make the lady unhappy, I'd have to pound your face in." He stuck the cigar back into his mouth. "I'm right fond of her."

Max studied him a moment, then laid his head back and laughed. "There's no way to win here. I think I finally figured that out."

"That's the first step." Trent shifted. "Since we've got a minute here without the ladies I thought you both should know that I finally got a report on this Hawkins character. Jasper Hawkins, smuggler, out of Miami. He's a known associate of our old friend Livingston."

"Well, well," Sloan murmured, crushing out the cigar.

"It begins to look like Livingston and

Caufield are one in the same. No sign of the boat yet."

"I've been thinking about that," Max put in. "It might be that they covered their tracks there. Even if they figured I was dead, they'd have to consider that the body would wash up eventually, be identified. Questions would be asked."

"So they ditched the boat," Trent mused.

"Or switched it." Max spread his hands. "They won't back off. I'm sure of that. Caufield, or whoever he is, is obsessed with the necklace. He'd change tactics, but he wouldn't give up."

"Neither will we," Trent murmured. The three men exchanged quiet looks. "If the necklace is in this house, we'll find it. And if that bastard —" He cut himself off as he spotted his wife racing through the doors at the far end of the terrace. "C.C." He was up quickly, starting toward her. "What's wrong? What are you doing home?"

"Nothing. Nothing's wrong." With a laugh, she threw her arms around him. "I love you."

"I love you, too." But he drew away to study her face. Her cheeks were flushed, her eyes brilliant and wet. "Well, it must be good news." He brushed her hair back, checking her brow as he did so. He knew she hadn't been feeling quite herself for the past week.

"The best." She glanced over at Sloan and Max. "Excuse us." Gripping Trent's hand, she pulled him down the terrace toward their room where she could tell him in private. Halfway there, she exploded. "Oh, I can't wait. I know I broke the sound barrier getting home after the test came in."

"What test? You're sick?"

"I'm pregnant." She held her breath, watching his face. Concern to shock, shock to wonder.

"You — pregnant?" He gaped down at her flat stomach, then back into her face. "A baby? We're having a baby?"

Even as she nodded, he was scooping her up, to swing her around and around as she clung to him.

"What the hell's with them?" Sloan wondered.

"Men." Behind Max, Lilah glided from another room. "You're all so dense." With a sigh, she laid a hand on Max's shoulder, watching her sister and Trent through misty eyes. "We're having a baby, you dummies."

"I'll be damned." After a whoop, Sloan

headed down to slap Trent on the back and kiss C.C. Hearing the sniffle behind him, Max rose.

"You okay?"

"Sure." She brushed a tear from her lashes, but another fell. "She's my baby sister." She sniffed again, then gave a watery laugh when Max offered her a handkerchief. "Trust you." She dabbed her eyes, blew her nose then sighed. "I'm going to keep it awhile, okay? We're all going to cry buckets when we go down and make the announcement to the rest of the family."

"That's all right." Unsure of himself, he stuck his hands into his pockets.

"Let's go down and see if there's any champagne in the fridge."

"Well, I think I should stay up here. Out of the way."

With a shake of her head, she took his hand firmly in hers. "Don't be a jerk. Like it or not, Professor, you're part of the family."

He let her lead him away and discovered he did like it. He liked it a lot.

*It was the stray puppy that started it. Such a poor, bedraggled little thing. Homeless and helpless. I have no idea how he found his way to the cliffs. Per-*

haps someone had disposed of an unwanted litter, or the pup had become separated from its mother. But we found him, Christian and I, on one of our golden afternoons. He was hiding in a huddle of rocks, half-starved and whimpering, a tiny black bundle of bones and scruffy black fur.

How patiently Christian lured him out, with a gentle voice and bits of bread and cheese. It touched me to see this sweetness in the man I love. With me, he is always tender, but I have seen the fierce impatience in him, for his art. I have felt the near-violent passion fighting for freedom when he holds me in his arms.

Yet with the puppy, the poor little orphan, he was instinctively kind. Perhaps sensing this, the pup licked his hand and allowed himself to be petted even after the meager meal had been gobbled down.

"A scrapper." Christian laughed as he took his beautiful artist's hands over the dirty fur. "Tough little fellow, aren't you?"

"He needs a bath," I said, but laughed as well when the dusty paws streaked my dress. "And a real meal." Delighted with the attention, the pup licked my face, his whole body trembling with delight.

*Of course, I fell in love. He was such a homely little bundle, so trusting, so needy. We played with him, as charmed as children, and had a laughing argument over what to call him.*

*We named him Fred. He seemed to approve as he yipped and danced and tumbled in the dirt. I will never forget the sweetness of it, the simplicity. My love and I sitting on the ground with a little lost pup, pretending that we would take him home together, care for him together.*

*In the end, I took Fred with me. Ethan had been asking for a pet, and I felt he was old enough now to be both appreciative and responsible. What a clamor there was when I brought the puppy to the nursery. The children were wide-eyed and excited, each taking turns holding and hugging until I'm sure young Fred felt like a king.*

*He was bathed and fed with a great deal of ceremony. Stroked and cuddled and tickled until he fell asleep in exhausted euphoria.*

*Fergus returned. The excitement over Fred had caused me to forget our plans for the evening. I'm sure my husband was right to be annoyed that I was far from ready to go out and dine. The children,* unable to contain their delight, raced about, adding to his impatience. Little Ethan, proud as a new father, carried Fred into the parlor.

"What the devil have you got?" Fergus demanded.

"A puppy." Ethan held the wriggling bundle up for his father's inspection. "His name is Fred."

Noting my husband's expression, I took the puppy from my son and began to explain how it had come about. I suppose I'd hoped to appeal to Fergus's softer side, to the love, or at least the pride he felt for Ethan. But he was adamant.

"I'll not have a mongrel in my house. Do you think I have worked all my life to own such things only to have some flea-ridden mutt relieving himself on the carpets, chewing on the draperies?"

"He'll be good." Lip quivering, Colleen hugged my skirts. "Please, Papa. We'll keep him in the nursery and watch him."

"You'll do no such thing, young lady." Fergus dismissed Colleen's tears with a glance and turned to Ethan, whose eyes were also brimming. There was a fractional softening in his expression. After all this was his first son, his heir, his immortality. "A mongrel's no pet for you, my lad.

Why any fisherman's son might own a mongrel. If it's a dog you want, we'll look into it when we get back to New York. A fine dog, with a pedigree."

"I want Fred." With his sweet face crumbling, Ethan looked up at his father. Even little Sean was crying now, though I doubt he understood.

"Out of the question." With his temper obviously straining, Fergus walked to the whiskey decanter and poured. "It's completely unsuitable. Bianca, have one of the servants dispose of it."

I know I paled as quickly as the children. Even Fred whimpered, pressing his face to my breast. "Fergus, you can't be so cruel."

There was surprise in his eyes, I have no doubt of it. It had never occurred to him that I would speak to him so, and in front of the children. "Madam, do as I bid."

"Mama said we could keep him," Colleen began, her youthful temper lifting her voice. "Mama promised. You can't take him away. Mama won't let you."

"I run this home. If you don't wish a strapping, mind your tone."

I found myself clutching Colleen's shoulders, as much to suppress her as to protect. He would not lift a hand to my children. Fury at the thought of it blinded me to all else. I know I trembled as I bent to her, to shift Fred back into her arms.

"Go upstairs to Nanny now," I said quietly. "Take your brothers."

"He won't kill Fred." Is there a rage more poignant than that of a child? "I hate him, and I won't let him kill Fred."

"Shh. It will be all right, I promise you. It will be all right. Go up to Nanny."

"A poor job you've done, Bianca," Fergus began when the children had left us. "The girl is old enough to know her place."

"Her place?" The fury had my heart roaring in my head. "What is her place, Fergus? To sit quietly in some corner, her hands folded, her thoughts and feelings unspoken until you have bartered her off into a suitable marriage? They are children. Our children. How could you hurt them so?"

Never in our marriage had I used such a tone with him. Never had I thought to. For a moment I was certain that he would strike me. It was in his eyes. But he seemed to pull himself back, though his fingers were white as marble against the glass he held.

*"You question me, Bianca?"* His face was very pale with his rage, his eyes very dark. *"Do you forget whose house you stand in, whose food you eat, whose clothes you wear?"*

*"No."* Now I felt a new kind of grief, that our marriage should be brought down to only that. *"No, I don't forget. I can't forget. I would sooner wear rags and starve than see you hurt my children so. I will not allow you to take that dog from them and have him destroyed."*

*"Allow?"* He was no longer pale, but crimson with fury. *"Now it is you who forget your place, Bianca. Is it any wonder the children openly defy me with such a mother?"*

*"They want your love, your attention."* I was shouting now, beyond restraint. *"As I have wanted it. But you love nothing but your money, your position."*

How bitterly we argued then. The names he called me I can't repeat. He dashed the glass against the wall, shattering the crystal and his own control. There was a wildness in his eyes when his hands came around my throat. I was afraid for my life, terrified for my children. He shoved me aside so that I fell into a chair. He was breathing quickly as he stared down at me.

Very slowly, with great effort, he composed himself. The violent color faded from his cheeks. "I can see now that I've been too generous with you," he said. "From this point, it will change. Don't think you will continue to go your own way as you choose. We will cancel our plans for this evening. I have business in Boston. While I'm there, I will interview governesses. It's time the children learned respect, and how to appreciate their position. Between you and their nanny, they have become spoiled and willful." He took his watch from his pocket and studied the time. "I will leave tonight and be gone two days. When I return I expect you to have remembered your duties. If the mongrel is still in my house when I return, both you and the children will be punished. Am I clear, Bianca?"

"Yes." My voice shook. "Quite clear."

"Excellent. In two days then."

He walked out of the parlor. I did not move for an hour. I heard the carriage come for him. Heard him instruct the servants. In that time my head had cleared and I knew what I had to do.

# Chapter Seven

"What the hell good is messing with all these papers?" Hawkins paced the sun-washed room in the rented house. He had never been a patient man and preferred to use his fists or a weapon rather than his brain. His associate, now going by the name of Robert Marshall, sat at an oak desk, carefully leafing through the papers he had stolen from The Towers a month before. He had dyed his hair a nondescript brown and had grown a credible beard and mustache that he tinted the same shade.

If Max Quartermain had seen him, he would have called him Ellis Caufield. Whatever name he chose, whatever disguise he employed, he was a thief whose unscrupulous mind had centered on the Calhoun emeralds.

"I went through a great deal of trouble to get these papers," Caufield said mildly. "Now that we've lost the professor, I'll have to decipher them myself. It will simply take a little longer."

"This whole job stinks." Hawkins stared out the window at the thick trees that sheltered the house. It was tucked behind a grove of quaking aspen, and the cool leaves quivered continually in the breeze. With the windows of the study thrown open, the scents of pine and sweet peas wafted into the room. He could only smell his own frustration. The bright glint of blue that was the bay didn't lift his mood. He'd spent enough time in prison to feel shut in, however lovely the surroundings.

Cracking his knuckles, he turned away from the view. "We could be stuck in this place for weeks."

"You should learn to appreciate the scenery. And the room." His partner's nervous habit was an annoyance, but he tolerated it. For the time being, he needed Hawkins. After the emeralds had been found . . . well, that was another matter. "I certainly prefer the house to the boat for the long term. And finding the right accommodations across the bay on this island was difficult and expensive."

"That's another thing." Hawkins pulled out a cigarette. "We're spending a bundle, and all we've got to show for it is a bunch of old papers."

"I assure you, the emeralds will be more than worth any overhead."

"If the bloody things exist."

"They exist." Caufield waved the smoke away in a fussy gesture, but his eyes were intense. "They exist. Before the summer ends, I'm going to hold them in my hands." He lifted them. They were smooth and white and clever. He could all but see the glittery green stones dripping from his palms. "They're going to be mine."

"Ours," Hawkins corrected.

Caufield looked up and smiled. "Ours, of course."

After dinner, Max went back to his lists. He told himself he was being responsible, doing what needed to be done. In truth he'd needed to put some distance between himself and Lilah. He couldn't delude himself into thinking it was only desire he felt for her. That was a basic biological re-action and could be triggered by a face on a television screen, a voice on the radio.

There was nothing so simple or so easily dismissed about his reaction to Lilah.

Every day he was around her his emotions became more tangled, more unsteady and more ungovernable. It had been diffi-cult enough when he had looked at her and wanted her. Now he looked at her and felt his needs meld with dreams that were unrealistic, foolish and impossible.

He'd never given much thought to falling in love, and none at all to marriage and family. His work had always been enough, filling the gaps nicely. He enjoyed women, and if he fell far short of being the Don Juan of Cornell, he had managed a few comfortable and satisfying relationships. Still, he'd never felt a burning need to race to the altar or to start building picket fences.

Bachelorhood had suited him, and when he had thought about the future, he had imagined himself getting crusty, perhaps taking up the pipe and buying a nice dog for companionship.

He was an uncomplicated man who lived a quiet life. At least until recently. Once he had helped the Calhouns locate the emeralds, he would go back to that quiet life. And he would go back alone. While things might never be exactly the same for him, he knew that she would forget the awkward college professor before the winter winds blew across the bay.

And he figured the sooner he finished what he had agreed to do and went away, the easier it would be to go. Gathering his lists, he decided it was time to take the next step toward ending the most incredible summer of his life.

He found Amanda in her room, going over her own lists. These were for her wedding, which would take place in three weeks.

"I'm sorry to interrupt."

"That's okay." Amanda pushed her glasses back up her nose and smiled. "I've got everything under control here except my nerves." She tapped her papers together and set them aside on the slant-top desk. "I was all for eloping, but Aunt Coco would have murdered me."

"I guess weddings take a lot of work."

"Even planning a small family ceremony is like plotting a major offensive. Or being in the circus," she decided, and laughed. "You end up juggling photographers with color schemes and fittings and floral arrangements. But I'm getting good at it. I took care of C.C.'s, I ought to be able to do the same for myself. Except . . ." Pulling her glasses off, she began to fold and unfold the earpieces. "The whole thing scares the good sense right out of me. So, take my mind off it, Max, and tell me what's on yours."

"I've been working on this. I don't know

how complete it is." He set his list in front of her. "The names of all the servants I could find, the ones who worked here the summer Bianca died."

Lips pursed, Amanda slid her glasses back on. She appreciated the precise handwriting and neat columns. "All of these?"

"According to the ledger I went through. I thought we could contact the families, maybe even luck out and find a few still alive."

"Anyone who worked here back then would have to be over the century mark."

"Not necessarily. A lot of the help could have been young. Some of the maids, the garden and kitchen help." When she began to tap her pencil on the desk, he shrugged. "It's a long shot, I know, but —"

"No." Her gaze still on the list, she nodded. "I like it. Even if we can't reach anyone who actually worked here then, they might have told stories to their children. It's a safe bet some of them were local — maybe still are." She looked up at him. "Good thinking, Max."

"I'd like to help you try to pin some of the names down."

"I can use all the help I can get. It's not going to be easy."

"Research is what I'm best at."

"You've got yourself a deal." She held out a hand to shake. "Why don't we split the list in half and start tomorrow? I imagine the cook, the butler, the house-keeper, Bianca's personal maid and the nanny all traveled with them from New York."

"But the day help, and the lower positions were hired locally."

"Exactly. We could divide the list in that way, then cross-reference . . ." She trailed off as Sloan came in through the terrace doors carrying a bottle of champagne and two glasses.

"Leave you alone for five minutes and you start entertaining other men in your room." He set the wine aside. "And talking about cross-referencing, too. Must be serious."

"We hadn't even gotten to alphabetizing," Amanda told Sloan.

"Looks like I got here just in time." He took the pencil out of her hand before drawing her to her feet. "In another minute you might have been hip deep in correlations."

They certainly didn't need him, Max decided. By the way they were kissing each other, it was apparent they'd forgotten all about him. On his way out, he cast one envious look over his shoulder. They were just smiling at each other, saying nothing. It was obvious that they were two people who knew what they wanted. Each other.

Back in his room, Max decided he would spend the rest of the evening working on notes for his book. Or, if he could gather up the courage, he could sit in front of the old manual typewriter Coco had unearthed for him. He could take that step, that big one, and begin writing the story instead of preparing to write it.

He took one look at the battered Remington and felt his stomach clutch. He wanted to sit down, to lay his fingers on those keys, just as desperately as a man wants to hold a loved and desired woman in his arms. He was as terrified of facing the single blank sheet of paper as he would have been of a firing squad. Maybe more so.

He just needed to prepare, Max told himself. His reference books needed to be positioned better. His notes had to be more easily accessible. The light had to be adjusted.

He thought of dozens of minute details to be perfected before he could begin. Once he had accomplished that, had tried and failed to think of more, he sat.

Here he was, he realized, about to begin something he'd dreamed of doing his entire life. All he had to do was write the first sentence, and he would be committed.

His fingers curled into fists on the keys.

Why did he think he could write a book? A thesis, a lecture, yes. That's what he was trained to do. But a book, God, a novel wasn't something anyone could be taught to do. It took imagination and wit and a sense of drama. Daydreaming a story and articulating it on paper were two entirely different things.

Wasn't it foolish to begin something that was bound to lead to failure? As long as he was preparing to write the book, there was no risk and no disappointment. He could go on preparing for years without any sense of shame. If he started it, really started it, there would be no more hiding behind notes and research books. When he failed, he wouldn't even have the dream.

Wound tight, he ran his fingers over the keys while his mind jumped with dozens of excuses to postpone the moment. When the first sentence streaked from his brain to his fingers and appeared on the blank sheet of paper, he let out a long, unsteady breath.

Three hours later, he had ten full sheets.

The story that had swum through his head for so long was taking shape with words. His words. He knew it was probably dreadful, but it didn't seem to matter. He was writing, actually writing. The process of it fascinated and exhilarated. The sound of it, the clatter and thud of the keys, delighted him.

He'd stripped off his shirt and shoes and sat bent over, his brows together, his eyes slightly unfocused. His fingers would race over the keys then stop while he strained to find the way to take what was in his head and put it on paper.

That was how Lilah found him. He'd left his terrace doors open for the breeze, though he'd long since stopped noticing it. The room was dark but for the slant of light from the lamp on the desk. She stood watching him, aroused by his total concentration, charmed by the way his hair fell into his eyes.

Was it any wonder she had come to him? she thought. She was so completely in love with him, how could she stay away? It couldn't be wrong to want to have a night with him, to show him that love in a way he might understand and accept. She needed to belong to him, to forge a bond that would matter to both of them.

Not sex, but intimacy. It had begun the moment he had lain half-drowned on the shingle and lifted a hand to her face. There was a connection she couldn't escape. And as she had risen from her own bed to come to his, one that she no longer wanted to escape.

Her instinct had led her to his room tonight as surely as it had led her to the beach during the storm.

The decision was hers, she knew. However badly he wanted her, he wouldn't take what wasn't offered. And he would hesitate to take even that because of his rules and his codes. Perhaps if he'd loved her . . . But she couldn't let herself think of that. In time, he would love her. Her own feelings were too deep and too strong not to find their match.

So she would take the first step. Seduction.

His concentration was so intense that a shout wouldn't have broken it. But her scent, whispering across the room on the night breeze, shattered it. Desire pumped into his blood before he glanced up and saw her in the doorway. The white robe fluttered around her. Caught in the fanning air, her hair danced over her shoulders. Behind her the sky was a black canvas, and she had — illusion to reality — stepped out of it. She smiled and his fingers went limp on the keys.

"Lilah."

"I had a dream." It was true, and speaking the truth helped calm her nerves. "About you and me. There was moonlight. I could almost feel the light on my skin until you touched me." She stepped inside, the movement causing the silk to make a faint shushing sound, like water rippling over water. "Then I didn't feel anything but you. There were flowers, the fragrance very light, very sweet. And a nightingale, that long liquid call for a mate. It was a lovely dream, Max." She stopped beside his desk. "Then I woke up, alone."

He was certain the ball of tension in his stomach would rip free any moment and leave him helpless. She was more beautiful than any fantasy, her hair like wildfire across her shoulders, her graceful body silhouetted enticingly beneath the thin, shifting silk.

"It's late." He tried to clear the huskiness from his throat. "You shouldn't be here."

"Why?"

"Because . . . it's —"

"Improper?" she suggested. "Reckless?" She brushed the hair from his brow. "Dangerous?"

Max lurched to his feet to grasp the back of the chair. "Yes, all of that."

There were age-old women's secrets in her eyes. "But I feel reckless, Max. Don't you?"

Desperate was the word. Desperate for just one touch. His fingers whitened on the chair back. "There's a matter of respect."

Her smile was suddenly very warm and very sweet. "I respect you, Max."

"No, I mean . . ." She looked so lovely when she smiled that way, so young, so fragile. "We decided to be friends."

"We are." With her eyes on his, she lifted her hand to smooth back her hair. Her rings glittered in the lamplight.

"And this is —"

"Something we both want," she finished. When she stepped toward him, he jerked back. The chair tumbled over. Her laughter wasn't mocking, but warm and delighted. "Do I make you nervous, Max?"

"That's a mild word for it." He could barely drag air through his dry throat. At his sides his hands were fisted, twins of the fists in the pit of his stomach. "Lilah, I don't want to ruin what we have together.

Lord knows I don't want you to break my heart."

She smiled, feeling a surge of hope through her own nerves. "Could I?"

"You know you could. You've probably lost track of the hearts you've broken."

There it was again, she thought as disappointment shuddered through her. He still saw her, would likely always see her, as the careless siren who lured men, then discarded them. He didn't understand that it was her heart on the line, had been her heart on the line all along. She wouldn't let it stop her — couldn't. Tonight, being with him tonight, was meant. She felt it too strongly to be wrong.

"Tell me, Professor, do you ever dream of me?" She stepped toward him; he backed up. Now they stood in the shadows beyond the lamplight. "Do you ever lie in the dark and wonder what it would be like?"

He was losing ground fast. His mind was so full of her there wasn't room for anything but need. "You know I do."

Another step and they were caught in a slash of moonlight as white as her robe, and as seductive. "And when you dream of it, where are we?"

"It doesn't seem to matter where." He

had to touch her, couldn't resist, even if it was only to brush his fingertips over her hair. "We're alone."

"We're alone now." She slid her hands over his shoulders to link them behind his neck. "Kiss me, Max. The way you did the first time, when we were sitting on the grass in the sunlight."

His fingers were in her hair, taut as wires. "It won't end there, Lilah. Not this time."

Her lips curved as they lifted to his. "Just kiss me."

He fought to gentle his grip, to keep his mouth easy as it cruised over hers. Surely he was strong enough to hold back this clawing need to ravage. He wouldn't hurt her. He swore it. And clung to the dim hope that he could have this one night with her and emerge unscathed.

So sweet, she thought. So lovely. The tenderness of the kiss was all the more poignant as she could feel the tremble of repressed passion in both of them. Her heart, already brimming with love, overflowed. When their lips parted, there were tears glittering in her eyes.

"I don't want it to end there." She touched her lips to his again. "Neither of us do."

"No."

"Make love with me, Max," she murmured. She kept her eyes on his as she stepped back, unbelting her robe. "I need you tonight." The robe slithered to the floor.

Beneath it her skin was as white and smooth as marble. Her long slender limbs might have been carved and polished by an artist's hands. She stood, cloaked only in moonlight, and waited.

He'd never seen anything more perfect, more elegant or fragile. Suddenly his hands felt big and clumsy, his fingers rough. His breath tore raggedly through his lips as he touched her. Though his fingers barely floated over her skin, he was terrified he would leave bruises behind. Fascinated, he watched his hand skim over her, tracing the slope of her shoulders, sliding down the graceful arms and back again. Carefully, very carefully, brushing over the water-soft skin of her breasts.

First her legs went weak. No one had ever touched her like this, with such drugging gentleness. It was as though she were the first woman he had ever seen and he was memorizing her face and form through his fingertips. She had come to seduce, yet her arms lay weighted at her sides. And she was seduced. Her head fell back in an involuntary gesture of surrender. He had no way of knowing that this surrender was her first.

That vulnerable column of her throat was impossible to resist. He pressed his mouth against it even as his palm brushed lightly over the point of her breast.

The combination had a bolt of sensation shooting through her. Stunned by it, she jolted and gasped out his name.

He retreated instantly, cursing himself. "I'm sorry." He was half-blind with needs and shook his head to clear it. "I've always been clumsy."

"Clumsy?" In a haze of longing, she swayed toward him, running her lips over his shoulder, his throat, down his chest. "Can't you feel what you're doing to me? Don't stop." Her mouth found his and lingered. "I think I'd die if you did."

The barrage on his system nearly felled him. Her hands streaked over him, impatient and greedy. Her mouth, Lord her mouth was hot and quick, searing his skin with every breathy kiss. He couldn't think, could barely breathe. There was nothing to do but feel.

Straining for control, he lifted her face to his, calming her lips, drugging them and her as he centered all of his needs into that one endless kiss. Yes, he could feel what he was doing to her, and it amazed him. On a low, throaty groan, she went limp in a surrender more erotic than any seduction. Her body seemed to melt into his in total pliancy, total trust. When he lifted her into his arms she made a small, lazy sound of pleasure.

Her eyes were nearly closed. He could see the glint of green under the cover of her lashes. As he carried her to the bed he felt as strong as Hercules. Gently, watching her face, he laid her on the covers.

There was moonlight here, streaming through the windows like liquid silver. He could hear the wind sighing through the trees and the distant drum of water on rock. Her scent, as mysterious as Eve, reached for him as easily as her arms.

He took her hands. Struck by the romance of the night, he brought them to his lips, skimming his mouth over her knuckles, down her fingertips, over her palms. All the time, he watched her as he scraped lightly with his teeth, soothed and aroused with his tongue. He heard her breath quicken, watched her eyes cloud with dazed pleasure and confusion as he made love to her hands. He felt the thunder of her pulse when he pressed his lips to her wrist.

He was bringing her something she hadn't prepared for. Total helplessness. Did he know how completely she was in his power? she wondered hazily. The drunk and weighty pleasure was flowing from her fingertips into every part of her. When his lips slid down her arm to nuzzle the inside of her elbow, a moan was wrenched from her.

She wasn't even aware that she was moving under him, inviting him to take anything, everything he wanted. When his mouth came to hers at last, his name was the only word she could form.

He fought back greed. It was impossible not to feel it, with her body so hot, so soft, so agile beneath his. But he refused to give in to it. Tonight, for there might only be tonight, would last. He wanted more than that fast and frantic union his body ached for. He wanted the dazzling pleasure of learning every inch of her, of discovering her secrets, her weaknesses. With patience he could brand in his brain what it was like to touch her and feel her tremble, what it was like to taste and hear her sigh. When her hands moved over him, he knew she was as lost in the night as he.

He slid down her slowly, searing her flesh with open-mouthed kisses, whispering fingertips. With torturous patience he lingered at her breasts until they were achingly full with pleasure. Down, gradually down, while her fingers clenched and unclenched in his hair. He could hear her now, soft, incoherent pleas, gasping sighs as he trailed his mouth down her torso, nipped teasing teeth across her hip. She felt his breath flutter against her thigh and cried out, rearing up as the first hot wave slammed into her. She flew over the edge then cartwheeled down as he roamed relentlessly to her knee.

He couldn't get enough. Every taste of her was more potent than the last. He sated himself on it as the tension began to roar in his temples, burn in his blood. Grasping her flailing hands, he drove himself mad by pushing her to peak again. When her body went lax, when her breath was sobbing, he brought his mouth back to hers.

She was willing to beg, but she couldn't speak. Sensation after sensation tore through her, leaving her weak and giddy and aching for more. Desperate for him, she fumbled with the catch of his jeans. She would have screamed with frustration if his mouth hadn't seduced hers into a groan.

Tugging, gasping, she dragged the denim over his hips, too delirious to know that her urgent fingers were making him shudder. Damp flesh slid over damp flesh as they pulled the jeans aside.

"Wait." The word came harshly through his lips as he fought to hold on to the last of his control. "Look at me." His fingers tightened in her hair as she opened her eyes. "Look at me," he repeated. "I want you to remember."

Muscles trembling with the effort to go slowly, he slipped into her. Her eyes went cloudy but remained on his as they set an easy rhythm. She knew as he filled her, with himself, with such perfect beauty, that she would always remember.

It was so sweet, so natural, the way his head rested between her breasts. Lilah smiled at the sensation as she stroked his hair. One hand was still linked with his as it had been when they'd slid over the crest together. Half-dreaming now, she imagined what it would be like to fall asleep together, just like this, night after night.

He could feel her relax beneath him, her body warm and pliant, her skin still sheened with the dew of passion. Her heartbeat was slowing gradually. For a moment he could pretend that this was one night among many. That she could belong to him in that complex and intimate way a woman belonged to a man.

He knew he'd given her pleasure, and that for a time they had been as bound together as two people could be. But now, he hadn't an idea what he should say — because all he wanted to say was that he loved her.

"What are you thinking?" she murmured.

He steadied himself. "My brain's not working yet."

Her laugh was low and warm. She shifted, wriggling down until they were face-to-face. "Then I'll tell you what I'm thinking." She brought her mouth to his in a languid, lingering kiss. "I like your lips." Teasingly she nipped the lower one. "And your hands. Your shoulders, your eyes." As she spoke, she trailed a fingertip up and down his spine. "In fact, at the moment I can't think of anything I don't like about you."

"I'll remind you of that the next time I irritate you." He combed her hair back because he enjoyed seeing it spread over his sheets. "I can't believe I'm here with you, like this."

"Didn't you feel it, Max, almost from the beginning?"

"Yes." He traced her mouth with a fingertip. "I figured it was wishful thinking."

"You don't give yourself enough credit, Professor." She traced light, lazy kisses over his face. "You're an attractive man with an admirable mind and a sense of compassion that's irresistible." Her eyes didn't light with amusement when he shifted. Instead she lay a hand on his cheek. "When you made love with me tonight, it was beautiful. The most beautiful night of my life."

She saw it in his eyes. Not embarrassment now, but plain disbelief. Because she was defenseless, stripped to the soul, nothing could have hurt her more. "Sorry," she said tightly and moved away. "I'm sure that sounds trite coming from me."

"Lilah . . ."

"No, it's fine." She pressed her lips together until she was certain her voice would be light and breezy again. "No use complicating things." As she sat up, she tossed her hair back. "There aren't any strings here, Professor. No trapdoors, no fine print. We're two consenting adults who enjoy each other. Agreed?"

"I'm not sure."

"Let's just say we'll take it a day at a time. Or a night at a time." She leaned over to kiss him. "Now that we've got that settled, I'd better go."

"Don't." He took her hand before she could slip off the bed. "Don't go. No strings," he said carefully as he studied her. "No complications. Just stay with me tonight."

She smiled a little. "I'll just seduce you again."

"I was hoping you'd say that." He pulled her against him. "I want you with me when the sun comes up."

# Chapter Eight

When the sun came up to pour golden light through the windows and chase away the last dusky shadows, she was in his arms. It seemed incredible to him that her head would be resting on his shoulder, her hand fisted lightly over his heart. She slept like a child, deeply, curled toward him for warmth and comfort.

Though the night was over, he lay still, loath to wake her. The birds had begun their morning chorus. It was so quiet, he could hear the wind breathing through the trees. He knew that soon the sound of saws and hammers would disrupt the peace and bring reality back. So he clung to this short interlude between the mystery of the night and the bustle of day.

She sighed and settled closer as he stroked her hair. He remembered how generous she had been in those dark sleepy hours. It seemed he had only to think, to wish, and she would turn toward him. Again and again they had loved, in silence and with perfect understanding.

He wanted to believe in miracles, to believe that it had been as special and monumental a night for her as it had been for him. He was afraid to take her words at face value.

*No one's ever made me feel the way you do.*

Yet they had played over and over in his head, giving him hope. If he was careful and patient and weighed each step before it was taken, maybe he could make a miracle.

Though he didn't feel suited to the role of prince, he tilted her face to his to wake her with a kiss.

"Mmm." She smiled but didn't open her eyes. "Can I have another?"

Her voice, husky with sleep, sent desire shivering along his skin. He forgot to be careful. He forgot to be patient. His mouth took hers the second time with an edgy desperation that had her system churning before she was fully awake.

"Max." Throbbing, she locked herself around him. "I want you. Now. Right now."

He was already inside her, already dragging her with him where they both wanted to go. The ride was fast and furious, shooting them both to the top where they clung, breathless and giddy.

When her hands slid off his damp back,

she still hadn't opened her eyes. "Good morning," she managed. "I just had the most incredible dream."

Though he was still light-headed, he braced on his forearms to look down at her. "Tell me about it."

"I was in bed with this very sexy man. He had big blue eyes, dark hair that was always falling in his face." Smiling, she opened her eyes and brushed it back for him. "This long, streamlined body." Still watching him, she moved her hands deliberately over him. "I didn't want to wake up, but when I did, it was even better than the dream."

Afraid he was crushing her, he rolled to reverse their positions. "What are the chances of spending the rest of our lives in this bed?"

She dropped a kiss on his shoulder. "I'm game." Then she groaned when the drone of power tools cut through the morning quiet. "It can't be seven-thirty."

As reluctant as she, he glanced at the clock beside the bed. "I'm afraid it can."

"Tell me it's my day off."

"I wish I could."

"Lie," she suggested, laying her cheek on his chest.

"Will you let me take you to work?"

She winced. "Don't say that word."

"Go for a drive with me after?"

She lifted her head again. "Where?"

"Anywhere."

Tilting her head, she smiled. "My favorite place."

Max kept his mind off Lilah — or tried to — by focusing on the multilayered task of locating people to go with the names on his list. He checked court records, police records, church records and death certificates. His meticulous legwork was rewarded with a handful of addresses.

When he felt he'd exhausted all the leads for that day, he drove by C.C.'s garage. He found her buried to the waist under the hood of a black sedan.

"I'm sorry to interrupt," he shouted over the din jingling out of a portable radio.

"Then don't." There was a streak of grease over her brow, but her scowl disappeared when she looked up and saw Max. "Hi."

"I could come back."

"Why, just because I snapped your head off?" She grinned, taking a rag out of her coveralls to wipe her hands. "Buy you a drink?" She jerked her head toward a soft drink machine.

"No, thanks. I just stopped by to ask you about a car."

"You're driving Lilah's, aren't you? Is it acting up?"

"No. The thing is I might be doing a lot of driving in the next few days, and I don't feel right using her car. I thought you might know if there's anything for sale in the area."

C.C. pursed her lips. "You want to buy a car?"

"Nothing extravagant. Just some convenient transportation. Then when I get back to New York . . ." He trailed off. He didn't want to think about going back to New York. "I can always sell it later."

"It so happens I do know somebody with a car for sale. Me."

"You?"

Nodding, she stuffed the rag back into her pocket. "With a baby coming, I've decided to turn in my Spitfire for a family car."

"Spitfire?" He wasn't sure what that was, but it didn't sound like the kind of car a dignified college professor would drive.

"I've had her for years, and I sure would feel better selling her to someone I know." She already had his hand and was pulling him outside.

There it sat, a fire-engine red toy with a white rag top and bucket seats. "Well, I . . ."

"I rebuilt the engine a couple of years ago." C.C. was busy opening the hood. "She drives like a dream. There's less than ten thousand miles on the tires. I'm the original owner, so I can guarantee she's been treated like a lady. And there's . . ." She glanced up and grinned. "I sound like a guy in a plaid sports jacket."

He could see his face in the shiny red paint. "I've never owned a sports car."

The wistfulness in his voice made C.C. smile. "Tell you what, leave me Lilah's car, drive her around. See how she suits you."

Max found himself behind the wheel, trying not to grin like a fool as the wind streamed through his hair. What would his students think, he wondered, if they could see sturdy old Dr. Quartermain tooling around in a flashy convertible? They'd probably think he'd gone around the bend. Maybe he had, but he was having the time of his life.

It was a car that would suit Lilah, he thought. He could already see her sitting beside him, her hair dancing as she laughed and lifted her arms to the wind.

Or kicked back in the seat, her eyes closed, letting the sun warm her face.

It was a nice dream, and it could come true. At least for a while. And maybe he wouldn't sell the car when he got back to New York. There was no law that said he had to drive a practical sedan. He could keep it to remind him of a few incredible weeks that had changed his life.

Maybe he'd never be sturdy old Dr. Quartermain again.

He cruised up the winding mountain roads, then back down again to try out the little car in traffic. Delighted with the world in general, he sat at a light, tapping his fingers against the wheel to the beat of the music on the radio.

There were people jamming the sidewalks, crowding the shops. If he'd seen a parking place, he might have whipped in, strolled into a shop himself just to test his endurance. Instead, he entertained himself by watching people scout for that perfect T-shirt.

He noticed the man with dark hair and a trim dark beard standing on the curb, staring at him. Full of himself and the spiffy car, Max grinned and waved. He was halfway down the block before it hit him. He braked, causing a bellow of bad-tempered honking. Thinking fast, he turned a sharp left, streaked down a side street and fought his way through traffic back to the intersection. The man was gone. Max searched the street but couldn't find a sign of him. He cursed low and bitterly over the lack of a parking space, over his own slow-wittedness.

The hair had been dyed, and the beard had hid part of the face. But the eyes . . . Max couldn't forget the eyes. It had been Caufield standing on the crowded sidewalk, looking at Max not with admiration or absent interest, but with barely controlled rage.

He had himself under control by the time he picked Lilah up at the visitors center. He had made what he considered the logical decision not to tell her. The less she knew, the less she was involved. The less she was involved, the better chance there was that she wouldn't be hurt.

She was too impulsive, he reflected. If she knew Caufield had been in the village, she would try to hunt him down herself. And she was too clever. If she managed to find him . . . The idea made Max's blood run cold. No one knew better than he how ruthless the man could be.

When he saw Lilah coming across the lot toward the car, he knew he'd risk anything, even his life, to keep her safe.

"Well, well, what's this?" Brows lifted, she tapped a finger on the fender. "My old heap wasn't good enough, so you borrowed my sister's?"

"What?" Foolishly he'd forgotten the car and everything else since he'd recognized Caufield. "Oh, the car."

"Yes, the car." She leaned over to kiss him, and was puzzled by his absent response and the pat on her shoulder.

"Actually, I'm thinking of buying it. C.C.'s in the market for a family car, so . . ."

"So you're going to buy yourself a snappy little toy."

"I know it's not my usual style," he began.

"I wasn't going to say that." Her brows drew together as she studied his face. Something was going on in that complicated mind of his. "I was going to say good for you. I'm glad you're giving yourself a break." She hopped in and stretched. Her lifted hand reached for his, but he only gave it a light squeeze, then released it. Telling herself she was being oversensitive, she fixed a smile in place. "So, how about that drive? I was thinking we could cruise down the coast."

"I'm a little tired." He hated lying, but he needed to get back to talk to Trent and Sloan, to feed the new description to the police. "Can I have a rain check?"

"Sure." She managed to keep her smile in place. He was so polite, so distant. Wanting some echo of their previous intimacy, she put a hand over his when he slipped into the car beside her. "I'm always up for a nap. Your room or mine?"

"I'm not . . . I don't think that's a good idea."

His hand was tense over the gearshift, and his fingers made no move to link with hers. He wouldn't even look at her, hadn't really looked at her, she realized, since she'd crossed the lot.

"I see." She lifted her hand from his and let it fall in her lap. "Under the circumstances, I'm sure you're right."

"Lilah —"

"What?"

No, he decided. He needed to do this his way. "Nothing." Reaching for the keys, he switched on the ignition.

They didn't speak on the way home. Max continued to convince himself that lying to her was the best way. Maybe she was miffed because he'd put off the drive, but he'd make it up to her. He just had to keep out of her way until he'd handled a few details. In any case his mind was crowded with possibilities that he needed time and space to work through. If Caufield and Hawkins were both still on the island, both of them bold enough to stroll through the village, did that mean they had found something useful in the papers? Were they still looking? Had they, as he had, dipped into the resources at the library to find out more?

They knew he was alive now. Would they manage to connect him with the Calhouns? If they considered him a liability, would his relationship with Lilah put her in danger?

That was a risk he couldn't afford to take.

He turned up the winding road that brought the peak of The Towers into view.

"I may have to go back to New York sooner than I expected," he said, thinking out loud.

To keep from protesting, she pressed her lips tight. "Really?"

He glanced over, cleared his throat. "Yes . . . ah, business. I could continue to do my research from there."

"That's very considerate of you, Professor. I'm sure you'd hate to leave a job half-done. And you wouldn't have any awkward relationships to interfere."

His mind was already focused on what needed to be done, and he made an absent sound of agreement.

By the time they pulled up at The Towers, Lilah had managed to turn the hurt into anger. He didn't want to be with her, and by his attitude it was plain he regretted that they'd ever been together. Fine. She wasn't about to sit around and sulk because some highbrow college professor wasn't interested in her.

She resisted slamming the car door, barely resisted biting his hand off at the wrist when he set it on her shoulder. "Maybe we can drive down the coast tomorrow."

She glanced at his hand, then at his face. "Don't hold your breath."

He jammed his hands into his pockets as she strolled up the steps. Definitely miffed, he thought.

By the time he had relayed his information to the other men and had fought his way through the pecking order at the police station, he really was tired. It might have been tension or the fact that he'd only had a couple hours' sleep the night before, but he gave in, stretched across his bed and tuned out until dinner.

Feeling better, he wandered downstairs. He thought about finding Lilah, asking her to walk in the gardens after the meal. Or maybe they'd take a drive after all, in the moonlight. It hadn't been a very big lie, and now that he'd unburdened himself to the police, he wouldn't have to dwell on it. In any case, if he decided it was best to leave, he might not have another evening with her.

Yes, a drive. Maybe he could ask her if she'd consider visiting him in New York — or just going away for a weekend somewhere. It didn't have to end, not if he started taking those careful steps.

He strolled into the parlor, found it empty and strolled out again. Just the two of them, watching the moon on the water, maybe pulling over to walk along the beach. He could begin to court her properly. He imagined she'd be amused by the term, but it was what he wanted to do.

He followed the sound of a piano into the music room. Suzanna was alone, playing for herself. The music seemed to match the expression in her eyes. There was a sadness in them, too deep for anyone else to feel. But when she saw him, she stopped and smiled.

"I didn't mean to interrupt."

"That's all right. It's time to get back to the real world anyway. Amanda took the kids into town so I was taking advantage of the lull."

"I was just looking for Lilah."

"Oh, she's gone."

"Gone?"

Suzanna was pushing back from the piano when Max barked the word and had her rising slowly. "Yes, she went out."

"Where? When?"

"Just a little while ago." Suzanna studied him as she crossed the room. "I think she had a date."

"A — a date?" He felt as though someone had just swung a sledgehammer into his solar plexus.

"I'm sorry, Max." Concerned, she laid a comforting hand on his. She didn't think she'd ever seen a man more miserably in love. "I didn't realize. She may have just gone out to meet friends, or to be by herself."

No, he thought, shaking his head. That would be worse. If she was alone, and Caufield was anywhere close . . . He shook off the panic. It wasn't Lilah the man was after, but the emeralds.

"It's all right, I only wanted to talk to her about something."

"Does she know how you feel?"

"No — yes. I don't know," he said lamely. He saw his romantic dreams about moonlight and courtship go up in smoke. "It doesn't matter."

"It would to her. Lilah doesn't take people or their feelings lightly, Max."

No strings, he thought. No trapdoors. Well, he'd already fallen through the trap- door, and his feelings were the noose around his neck. But that wasn't the point. "I'm just concerned about her going out alone. The police haven't caught Hawkins or Caufield yet."

"She went out to dinner. I can't see anyone popping up in a restaurant and de- manding emeralds she doesn't have." Suzanna gave his hand a friendly squeeze. "Come on, you'll feel better when you've eaten. Aunt Coco's lemon chicken should be about ready."

He sat through dinner, struggling to pre- tend that he had an appetite, that the empty place at the table didn't bother him. He discussed the progress of the servant's list with Amanda, dodged Coco's request to read his cards and felt generally miserable. Fred, sitting on his left foot, benefited from his mood by gobbling up the morsels of chicken Max slipped to him.

He considered driving into town, casually cruising, stopping at a few clubs and restaurants. But decided that would make him look like as big a jerk as he felt. In the end he retreated to his room and lost himself in his book.

The story didn't come as easily as it had the night before. Now it was mostly fits and starts with a lot of long pauses. Still he found even the pauses constructive as an hour passed into two, and two into three. It wasn't until he glanced at his watch and saw it was after midnight that he realized he hadn't heard Lilah come home. He'd deliberately left his door ajar so that he would know when she passed down the hall.

There was a good chance he'd been engrossed in his work and hadn't noticed when she'd walked by to her room. If she'd gone out to dinner, surely she'd be home by now. No one could eat for five hours. But he had to know.

He went quietly. There was a light in Suzanna's room, but the others were dark.

At Lilah's door, he hesitated, then knocked softly. Feeling awkward, he put his hand on the knob. He'd spent the night with her, he reminded himself. She could hardly be offended if he looked in to see if she was asleep.

She wasn't. She wasn't even there. The bed was made; the old iron head- and footboards that had probably belonged to a servant had been painted a gleaming white. The rest was color, so much it dazzled the eyes.

The spread was a patchwork quilt, expertly made from scraps of fabrics. Polka dots, checks, stripes, faded reds and blues. It was piled high with pillows of varied shapes and sizes. The kind of bed, Max thought, a person could sink into and sleep the day away. It suited her.

The room was huge, as most were in The Towers, but she'd cluttered it and made it cozy. On the walls that were painted a dramatic teal were sketches of wildflowers. The bold signature in the corners told him she'd done them herself. He hadn't even known she could draw. It made him realize there was quite a bit he didn't know about the woman he was in love with.

After closing the door behind him, he

wandered the room, looking for pieces of her.

A baker's rack was packed with books. Keats and Byron jumbled with grisly murder mysteries and contemporary romances. A little sitting area was grouped in front of one of her windows, a blouse tossed carelessly over the back of a Queen Anne chair, earrings and glittering bracelets scattered over a Hepplewhite table. There was a bowl of smooth gemstones beside a china penguin. When he picked the bird up, it played a jazzy rendition of "That's Entertainment."

She had candles everywhere, in everything from elegant Meissen to a tacky reproduction of a unicorn. Dozens of pictures of her family were scattered throughout. He picked up one framed snapshot of a couple, arms around each other's waists as they laughed into the camera. Her parents, he thought. Lilah's resemblance to the man, Suzanna's to the woman were strong enough to make him certain of it.

When the cuckoo in the clock on the wall jumped out, he jolted and realized it was twelve-thirty. Where the hell was she?

Now he paced, from the window where she'd hung faceted crystals to the brass urn filled with dried flowers, from bookcase to bureau. Nerves humming, he picked up an ornate cobalt bottle to sniff. And smelled her. He set it down hastily when the door opened.

She looked . . . incredible. Her hair windblown, her face flushed. She wore some sheer drapey dress that swirled around her legs in bleeding colors. Long multicolored columns of beads danced at her ears. She lifted a brow and closed the door.

"Well," she said. "Make yourself at home."

"Where the hell have you been?" The demand shot out, edged with frustration and worry.

"Did I miss curfew, Daddy?" She tossed a beaded bag onto the bureau. She'd lifted a hand to remove an earring when he whirled her around.

"Don't get cute with me. I've been worried sick. You've been out for hours. No one knew where you were." Or who you were with, he thought, but managed to bite that one back.

She jerked her arm free. He saw the temper flash hot into her eyes, but her voice was cool and slow and unmoved. "It may surprise you, Professor, but I've been going out on my own for a long time."

"It's different now."

"Oh?" Deliberately she turned back to the bureau. Taking her time, she unfastened an earring. "Why?"

"Because we . . ." Because we're lovers. "Because we don't know where Caufield is," he said with more control. "Or how dangerous he might be."

"I've also been looking out for myself for a long time." Deceptively sleepy, her eyes met his in the mirror. "Is the lecture over?"

"It's not a lecture, Lilah, I was worried. I have a right to know your plans."

Still watching him, she slid bracelets from her arms. "Just how do you figure that?"

"We're — friends."

The smile didn't reach her eyes. "Are we?"

He jammed impotent hands into his pockets. "I care about you. And after what happened last night, I thought we . . . I thought we meant something to each other. Now, twenty-four hours later you're out with someone else. Looking like that."

She stepped out of her shoes. "We went to bed last night, and enjoyed it." She nearly choked over the bitterness lodged in her throat. "As I recall we agreed there'd be no complications." Tilting her head, she studied him. Her easy shrug masked the fact that her hands were balled tight. "Since you're here, I suppose we could arrange a repeat performance." Her voice a purr, she stepped closer to run a finger down the front of his shirt. "That's what you want from me, isn't it, Max?"

Furious, he pushed her hand aside. "I don't care to be the second act of the evening."

The flush vanished, leaving her cheeks pale before she turned away. "Congratulations," she whispered. "Direct hit."

"What do you want me to say? That you can come and go as you please, with whomever you please, and I'll sit up and beg for the scraps from the table?"

"I don't want you to say anything. I just want you to leave me alone."

"I'm not going anywhere until we've straightened this out."

"Fine." The cuckoo chirped out again as she unzipped her dress. "Stay as long as you like. I'm getting ready for bed."

She stepped out of the dress, tossed it aside, then walked over to her vanity in a lacy, beribboned chemise. Sitting, she picked up her brush to drag it through her hair.

"What are you so angry about?"

"Angry." She set her teeth as she slapped the bristles against her scalp. "What makes you think I'm angry? Just because you're waiting for me in my room, incensed that I had the nerve to make plans of my own when you didn't have the time or inclination to spend an hour with me. Unless it was in the sack."

"What are you talking about?" He took her arm, then yelped when she rapped the brush hard on his knuckles.

"I'll let you know when I want to be touched."

He swore, grabbed the brush and tossed it across the room. Too enraged to see the surprise in her eyes, he hauled her to her feet. "I asked you a question."

She cocked her chin. "If you've finished your temper tantrum —" He nearly lifted her off her feet.

"Don't push," he said between his teeth.

"You hurt me." The words exploded out of her. "Last night, even this morning, I was worth a little of your time and attention. As long as there was sex. Then this afternoon, you couldn't even look at me. You couldn't wait to dump me off here and get away from me."

"That's crazy."

"That's just what happened. Damn you,

you made up lame excuses and practically patted me on the head. And tonight, you've got an itch and you're annoyed that I wasn't here to scratch it."

He was as pale as she now. "Is that what you think of me?"

She sighed then, and the anger dropped out of her voice. "It's what you think of me, Max. Now let me go."

His grip loosened so that she slipped away. "I had something on my mind this afternoon. It wasn't that I didn't want to spend time with you."

"I don't want excuses." She went to the terrace doors to fling them open. Maybe the wind would blow the tears away. "You've made it clear how you feel."

"Obviously I haven't. The last thing I wanted to do was hurt you, Lilah." But he'd lied to her, he thought. That had been his first mistake. "Just before I came to pick you up, I saw Caufield in the village."

She spun around. "What? You saw him? Where?"

"I was waiting at a light, and I saw him on the sidewalk. He's dyed his hair and grown a beard. By the time I'd realized, I was caught up in traffic and had to double back. He was gone."

"Why didn't you tell me you'd seen him?"

"I didn't want to worry you, and I wasn't going to have you getting some lame-brained idea about hunting him up yourself. You have a habit of acting on impulse, and I —"

"You jerk." The flush was back in her cheeks when she stepped forward to give him a shove. "That man is determined to take something from my family, and you don't have the sense to tell me you've seen him a few miles from here. If I'd known I might have been able to find him."

"Exactly my point. I'm not having you involved any more than necessary. That's why I thought it might be best if I went back to New York. They know I'm here now, and I'm not having you caught in the middle."

"You're not having?" She would have shoved him again, but he caught both her hands.

"That's right. You're going to stay out of it."

"Don't tell me —"

"I am telling you," he interrupted, pleased when she gaped at him. "What's more, you're not going to go wandering off at night until he's in custody. After I thought it over, I decided it was best if I stayed close and watched out for you. I'm going to take care of you whether you like it or not."

"I don't like it, and I don't need to be taken care of."

"Nonetheless." And he considered the argument closed.

It was her turn to stutter. "Why, you arrogant, self-important —"

"That's enough," he said in his best professor's voice and had her blinking. "There's no use arguing when the most intelligent decision's been made. Now, I think it's best if I take you to work every day. Whenever you make other plans, you'll let me know."

Her anger turned to simple shock. "I will not."

"Yes," he said mildly, "you will." He moved her hands behind her back to bring her closer. "About tonight," he began when their bodies brushed. "Clearly, you're laboring under a misconception concerning my motives, and my feelings."

She arched back, more surprised than annoyed when he didn't release her. "I don't want to talk about it."

"No, you prefer yelling about it, but that's unconstructive, and not my style." Both his hands and his voice were very firm. "To be precise, I didn't come here because I had an itch, though I certainly have every intention of making love with you."

Baffled, she stared at him. "What the devil's gotten into you?"

"I've suddenly realized that the best way to handle you is the way I handle difficult students. It takes more than patience. It requires a firm hand and a clear-cut outline of intentions and goals."

"A difficult —" She took a deep breath to hold on to her temper. "Max, I think you'd better go take some aspirin and lie down."

"As I was saying." He whispered a kiss over her cheek. "It isn't just a matter of sex, despite the fact that that aspect is incredibly satisfying. It's more of a matter of my being completely bewitched by you."

"Don't," she said weakly when he leaned close to nip at her ear.

"Maybe I've made the mistake of indicating that it's only the way you look, the way you feel under my hands, the way you taste that attracts me." He drew her bottom lip into his mouth, sucking gently until her eyes unfocused. "But it's more than that. I just don't know how to tell you." Her pulse beat fast and hard against his hands as he walked her backward.

"There's never been anyone like you in my life. I intend to keep you there, Lilah."

"What are you doing?"

"I'm taking you to bed."

She struggled to clear her head as his lips skimmed down her throat. "No, you're not." She was angry with him about something. But the reason floated just out of reach as his mouth seduced her.

"I need to show you how I feel about you." Still toying with her lips, he lowered her to the mattress.

Her hands were free now and slipped under his shirt to run along the warm flesh beneath. She didn't want to think. There were so many feelings to be absorbed, and she drew him closer, eager.

"I was jealous," he murmured as he slid one lacy strap from her shoulder and replaced it with his mouth. "I don't want another man touching you."

"No." He was touching her now, long, lingering strokes up and down her trembling body. "Just you."

He sank into a kiss, spinning it out, wallowing in the flavor, the texture, until he was drunk on it. Then, like an addict, he went back for more.

This was comfort and care and romance, she thought hazily. To float together like this, with a sweet breeze blowing over heated bodies, soft murmurs muffled against clinging lips. Desire so perfectly balanced with affection. Nothing mattered so much as this — holding on to the hope of love.

She lifted his shirt over his head and let her hands roam. He was strong. It was more than the subtle ridge of muscles over his back and shoulders. It was the strength inside that aroused her. The integrity, the dedication to do what was right. He would be strong enough to be loyal and honest and gentle with those he loved.

He shifted her so that she was cocooned by pillows. Kneeling beside her, he began to untie each tiny ribbon down the center of the ivory silk. The contrast of patient fingers and hungry eyes left her breathless. He parted the material, caressing the newly exposed flesh with his lips. It amazed and humbled him that her skin should be as soft as the silk.

As patiently as he, she undressed him. Though the need to hurry was clawing at both of them, they held back, the understanding spoken.

She rose, wrapping her arms around his neck until they were torso to torso, thigh to thigh. With the bright light showering around them, they explored each other. A shudder then a sigh, a request and an answer. Questing lips sought out new secrets. Eager hands discovered new pleasures.

When she locked herself around him, he filled her. Glorying in the sensation, she arched back, taking him deeper, gasping out his name as the first shock waves struck. He could see her, her willowy body bowed, her skin glowing in the light while her bright hair rained down her back. As she shuddered, the stunned pleasure rushed into her face.

Then his vision grayed, his own body trembled. His hands slid down to grip her hips. She was wrapped tight around him when they shot over the peak together.

# *Chapter Nine*

Max was whistling as he poured his coffee. It was the penguin's natty little tune and suited his mood. He had plans. Big ones. A drive along the coast, dinner at some out-of-the-way spot, then a nice long walk on the beach.

He sipped, scalded his tongue and grinned.

He was having a romance.

"Well, it's nice to see someone in such a bright mood so early in the morning." Coco sailed into the kitchen. She'd dyed her hair a raven black the night before, and the result had put her in a cheerful state of mind. "How about some blueberry pancakes?"

"You look terrific."

She beamed and reached for a frilly apron. "Why, thank you, dear. A woman needs a change now and again, I always say. Keeps men on their toes." After taking a large mixing bowl from the cupboard, she glanced back at him. "I must say, Max, you're looking rather well yourself this morning. The sea air or . . . something must agree with you."

"It's wonderful here. I'll never be able to thank you enough for letting me stay."

"Nonsense." In her haphazard way she began dumping ingredients into the bowl. It never failed to amaze Max how anyone could cook so carelessly with such exquisite results. "It was meant, you know. I knew it the moment Lilah brought you home. She was always one for bringing things home. Wounded birds, baby rabbits. Even a snake once." The memory of that made her pat her breast. "This was the first time she brought in an unconscious man. But that's Lilah," she continued, gaily mixing as she talked. "Always the unexpected. Quite talented, too. She knows all those Latin terms for weeds and the migratory habits of birds and things. When she's in the mood, she can draw beautifully."

"I know. I saw the sketches in her room."

She slanted him a look. "Did you?"

"I . . ." He took a quick gulp of coffee. "Yes. Do you want a cup?"

"No, I'll have my coffee when this is done." Oh, my, my, she thought, things were moving along just beautifully. The cards didn't lie. "Yes, our Lilah's quite a fascinating girl. Headstrong like the others, but in such a casual, deceptively amiable sort of way. I've always said that the right sort of man would recognize how special she is." Keeping an eye on Max, she rinsed and drained blueberries. "He'd need to be patient, but not malleable. Strong enough to keep her from veering off course too far, and wise enough not to try to change her." Gently folding the berries into the batter she smiled. "But then, if you love someone why would you want to change her?"

"Aunt Coco, are you pumping poor Max?" Lilah strolled in, yawning.

"What a thing to say." Coco heated the griddle and clucked her tongue. "Max and I were having a nice conversation. Weren't we, Max?"

"It certainly was a fascinating one."

"Really?" Lilah took the cup from him, and since he didn't make the move, leaned over to kiss him good morning. Watching, Coco all but rubbed her hands together. "I'll take that as a compliment, and since I see blueberry pancakes on the horizon, I won't complain."

Because the kiss had delighted her, Coco hummed as she got out dishes. "You're up early."

"It's becoming a habit of mine." Sipping

Max's coffee, Lilah sent him a lazy smile. "I'll have to break it soon."

"The rest of the brood will be trooping down any minute." And Coco liked nothing better than to have all of her chicks in one place. "Lilah, why don't you set the table?"

"I'll definitely have to break it." With a sigh, she handed Max back his coffee. But she kissed Coco's cheek. "I like your hair. Very French."

With what sounded almost like a giggle, Coco began to spoon up batter. "Use the good china, dear. I feel like celebrating."

Caufield hung up the phone and went into a small, nasty rage. He pounded the desk with his fists, tore a few pamphlets to bits and ended by smashing a crystal bud vase against the wall. Because he'd seen the mood before, Hawkins hung back until it passed.

After three calming breaths, Caufield sat back. The glaze of blank violence faded from his eyes as he steepled his fingers. "We seem to be victims of fate, Hawkins. The car our good professor was driving is registered to Catherine Calhoun St. James."

On an oath, Hawkins heaved his bulk away from the wall. "I told you this job stinks. By rights he should be dead. Instead he plops right down in their laps. He'll have told them everything by now."

Caufield tapped the tips of his fingers together. "Oh, assuredly."

"And if he recognized you —"

"He didn't." Exercising control, Caufield laced his fingers then laid them on the desk. "He never would have waved in my direction. He doesn't have the wit for it." Feeling his fingers tighten, he deliberately relaxed them. "The man's a fool. I learned more in one year on the streets than he in all of his years in higher institutions. After all, we're here, not on the boat."

"But he knows," Hawkins insisted, viciously cracking his knuckles. "Now they all know. They'll take precautions."

"Which only adds spice to the game and it's time to begin playing. Since Dr. Quartermain has joined the Calhouns, I believe I'll pay one of the ladies a call."

"You're out of your mind."

"Have a care, old friend," Caufield said mildly. "If you don't like my rules, there's nothing holding you here."

"I'm the one who paid for the damn boat." Hawkins dragged a hand through his short wiry hair. "I've put over a month in this job already. I've got an investment."

"Then leave it to me to make it pay off."
Thinking, Caufield rose to go to the
window. There were pretty summer flowers
in neat borders just outside. It reminded
him that he'd come a long way from the
tenements of south Chicago. With the emeralds, he'd go even further.

Perhaps a nice villa in the South Seas
where he could relax and refresh himself
while Interpol ran in circles looking for
him. He already had a new passport, a new
background, a new name in reserve — and
a tidy sum gathering interest in a discreet
Swiss account.

He'd been in the business most of his
life, quite successfully. He didn't need the
emeralds for the percentage of their value
he'd cull by fencing them. But he wanted
them. He intended to have them.

As Hawkins paced and abused his
knuckles, Caufield continued to gaze out
of the window. "Now, as I recall, during
my brief friendship with the lovely
Amanda, she mentioned that her sister
Lilah knew the most about Bianca. Perhaps she knows the most about the emeralds, as well."

This, at least, made some sense to
Hawkins. "Are you going to grab her?"

Caufield winced. "That's your style,

Hawkins. Credit me with a little more finesse. I believe I'll pay a visit to Acadia. They say the naturalist tours are very informative."

Lilah had always preferred the long, sunny days of summer. Though she felt there was something to be said for the long stormy nights of winter, as well. In truth, it was time she preferred. She didn't wear a watch. Time was something to be appreciated just for its existence, not as something to keep track of. But for the first time in her memory, she wished time would hurry.

She missed him.

It didn't matter how foolish it made her feel. She was in love and giddy with it. When the feeling was so strong, she resented every hour they weren't together.

It was stronger. She had fallen in love with his sweetness, his basic goodness. She had recognized his insecurity and, as she had with broken wings and damaged paws, had wanted to fix it.

She still loved all of those things, but now she had seen a different side of him. He'd been — masterful. She cringed at the term that entered her head and would have sworn she found it offensive. But it hadn't been offensive, not in Max. It had been illuminating.

He had taken charge. He had taken her, she thought with a quick flash of excitement. Though she still resented being compared to a difficult student, she had to admire his technique. He'd simply stated his intentions and moved on them.

She'd be the first to admit that she'd have frozen another man in his tracks with a few well-chosen words if he'd attempted the same thing. But Max wasn't any other man.

She hoped he was beginning to believe it.

While her mind wandered, she kept an eye on her group. Jordan Pond was a favored spot and she had a full load.

"Please, don't disturb the plant life. I know the flowers are tempting, but we have thousands of visitors who'll want to enjoy them, in their natural setting. The bottle-shaped flower you see in the pond is yellow cow lily, or spatterdock. The leaves floating on the surface are bladderwort, and common to most Acadia ponds. It is their tiny bladders that help the plant float, and that trap small insects."

In his ripped jeans and tattered backpack, Caufield listened to her lecture. Behind his dark glasses, his eyes were watchful. He paid attention, though the talk of bog and pond plants meant nothing to him. He held back a sneer when the group gasped as a heron glided overhead to wade in the shallows several yards away.

As if fascinated, he lifted the camera strapped around his neck and snapped pictures of the bird, the wild orchards, even of a bullfrog who had come out to bask on a floating leaf.

Most of all, he bided his time.

She continued to lecture, tirelessly answering questions as they moved along the trail beside the glassy water. She spelled a weary mother by hitching a toddler on her hip and pointing out a family of black ducks.

When the lecture was over, the group was free to follow the circular trail around the pond or retreat to their cars.

"Miss Calhoun?"

Lilah glanced around. She'd noticed the bearded hiker in the group, though he hadn't asked any questions during the lecture. There was a hint of the South in his voice.

"Yes?"

"I wanted to tell you how terrific your talk was. I teach high school geography and reward myself every summer with a trip through a national park. You're really one of the best guides I've come across."

"Thank you." She smiled, and though it was a natural gesture for her, felt reluctant to offer her hand. She didn't recognize the sweaty, bearded hiker, but she picked up something disturbing. "You'll have to visit the Nature Center while you're here. Enjoy your stay."

He put a hand on her arm. It was a casual move, far from demanding, but she disliked it intensely.

"I was hoping you could give me a little one-on-one, if you've got a minute. I like to give the kids a full-scale report when school starts in the fall. A lot of them never see the inside of a park."

She forced herself to shake off the mood. It was her job, she reminded herself, and she appreciated talking to someone with a genuine interest. "I'd be happy to answer any questions."

"Great." He pulled out a notebook he'd been careful to scribble in.

She relaxed a little, giving him a more in-depth talk than the average group required.

"This is so kind of you. I wonder, could I buy you some coffee, or a sandwich?"

"That isn't necessary."

"But it would be a pleasure."

"I have plans, but thanks."

He kept his smile in place. "Well, I'll be around for a few more weeks. Maybe some other time. I know this is going to sound strange, but I'd swear I'd seen you before. Have you ever been to Raleigh?"

Her instincts were humming, and she wanted to get away from him. "No, I haven't."

"It's the darnedest thing." As if puzzled, he shook his head. "You seem so familiar. Well, thanks again. I'd better start back to camp." He turned, then stopped. "I know. The papers. I've seen your picture. You're the woman with the emeralds."

"No. I'm afraid I'm the woman without them."

"What a story. I read about it down in Raleigh a month or two ago, and then . . . well, I have to confess, I'm just addicted to those supermarket tabloids. Comes from living alone and reading too many essays." He gave her a sheepish smile that would have charmed her if her senses hadn't been working overtime.

"I guess the Calhouns have been lining a lot of bird cages lately."

He rocked back on his heels and

laughed. "Pays to keep a sense of humor. I guess it's a hassle, but it gives people like me a lot of vicarious excitement. Missing emeralds, jewel thieves."

"Treasure maps."

"There's a map?" His voice sharpened and he worked hard at easing it again. "I hadn't heard."

"Sure, you can pick them up in the village." She reached in her pocket and drew the latest one out. "I've been collecting them. A lot of people are spending hard-earned money only to find out too late that $x$ doesn't mark the spot."

"Ah." He had to fight against clenching his jaw. "Capitalism."

"You bet. Here, a souvenir." She handed it to him, careful for reasons she couldn't quite place not to brush his fingers. "Your students might get a kick out of it."

"I'm sure they will." To give himself time, he folded it and slipped it into his pocket. "I really am fascinated by the whole thing. Maybe we can have that sandwich soon and you can give me a firsthand account of what it's like to look for buried treasure."

"Mostly, it's tedious. Enjoy your stay in the park."

Knowing there was no safe way to detain

her, he watched her go. She had a long, graceful body, he noted. He certainly hoped he wouldn't have to damage it.

"You're late." Max met her on the trail when she was still twenty yards from the parking area.

"It seems to be my day for teachers." She leaned into the kiss, pleased with how warm and solid it was. "I was detained by a Southern gentleman who wanted information on flora for his geography class."

"I hope he was bald and fat."

She didn't quite manage the laugh and rubbed the chill from her arms instead. "No, actually, he was quite trim and had an abundance of hair. But I turned down his request that I become the mother of his children."

"Did he make a pass at you?"

"No." She held a hand up before he could rush by her. And did laugh. "Max, I'm kidding — and if I wasn't, I can dodge passes all by myself."

He didn't feel as foolish as he might have even a day before. "You haven't been dodging mine."

"I can intercept them, too. Now what's behind your back?"

"My hands."

She laughed again and gave him a delighted kiss. "What else?"

He held out a clutch of painted daisies. "I didn't pick them," he said, knowing her feelings. "I bought them from Suzanna. She said you had a weakness for them."

"They're so cheerful," she murmured, absurdly touched. She buried her face in them, then lifted it to his. "Thanks."

As they began to walk, he draped an arm around her shoulders. "I bought the car from C.C. this afternoon."

"Professor, you're full of surprises."

"I thought you might like to hear about the progress Amanda and I are making on those lists. We could drive down the coast, have some dinner. Be alone."

"It sounds wonderful, but my flowers'll wilt."

He grinned down at her. "I bought a vase. It's in the car."

When the sun was setting behind the hills to the west, they walked along a cobble beach that formed a natural seawall on the southern point of the island. The water was calm, barely murmuring over the mounds of smooth stones. With the approach of dusk, the line between the sky and sea blurred until all was a soft, deep blue. A single gull, heading home, soared overhead with one long, defiant cry.

"This is a special place," Lilah told him. With her hand in his, she walked down the slope of cobbles to stand close to the verge of water. "A magic one. Even the air's different here." She closed her eyes to take a deep breath of it. "Full of stored energy."

"It's beautiful." Idly he bent to pick up a rock, just to feel the texture. In the near distance an island melted into the twilight.

"I often drive down here, just to stand and feel. I think I must have been here before."

"You just said you'd been here before."

Her eyes were soft and dreamy as she smiled. "I mean a hundred years ago, or five hundred. Don't you believe in reincarnation, Professor?"

"Actually, I do. I did a paper on it in college and after completing the research, I found it was a very viable theory. When you apply it to history —"

"Max." She framed his face with her hands. "I'm crazy about you." Her lips were curved when they met his, curved still when she drew away.

"What was that for?"

"Because I can see you, waist deep in thick books and cramped notes, your hair falling into your face and your eyebrows all drawn together the way they get when you're concentrating, doggedly pursuing truth."

Frowning, he tossed the cobble from hand to hand. "That's a pretty boring image."

"No, it's not." She tilted her head, studying him. "It's a true one, an admirable one. Even courageous."

He gave a short laugh. "Boxing yourself into a library doesn't take courage. When I was a kid, it was a handy escape. I never had an asthma attack reading a book. I used to hide there, in books," he continued. "It was fun imagining myself sailing with Magellan, or exploring with Lewis and Clark, dying at the Alamo or marching across a field at Antietam. Then my father would . . ."

"Would what?"

Uncomfortable, he shrugged. "He'd hoped for something different. He was a high school football star. Wide receiver. Played semipro for a while. The kind of man who's never been sick a day in his life. Likes to toss back a few beers on Saturday night and hunt on weekends during the season. I'd start wheezing as soon as he put a thirty-thirty in my hands." He tossed the cobble aside. "He wanted to make a man out of me, and never quite managed it."

"You made yourself." She took his hands, feeling a trembling anger for the man who hadn't appreciated or understood the gift he'd been given. "If he isn't proud of you, the lack is in him, not in you."

"That's a nice thought." He was more than a little embarrassed that he'd pulled those old, raw feelings out. "In any case, I went my own way. I was a lot more comfortable in a classroom than I was on a football field. And the way I figure it, if I hadn't hidden in the library all those years, I wouldn't be standing here with you right now. This is exactly where I want to be."

"Now that's a nice thought."

"If I tell you you're beautiful, are you going to hit me?"

"Not this time."

He pulled her against him, just to hold her as night fell. "I need to go to Bangor for a couple of days."

"What for?"

"I located a woman who worked as a

maid at The Towers the year Bianca died. She's living in a nursing home in Bangor, and I made arrangements to interview her." He tilted Lilah's face to his. "Come with me."

"Just give me time to rearrange my schedule."

*When the children were asleep, I told Nanny of my plans. I knew she was shocked that I would speak of leaving my husband. She tried to soothe. How could I explain that it wasn't poor Fred who had caused my decision. The incident had made me realize how futile it was to remain in an unhappy and stifling marriage. Had I convinced myself that it was for the children? Their father didn't see them as children who needed to be loved and coddled, but as pawns. Ethan and Sean he would strive to mold in his image, erasing every part of them he considered weak. Colleen, my sweet little girl, he would ignore until such time as he could marry her for profit or status.*

*I would not have it. Fergus, I knew, would soon wrench control from me. His pride would demand it. A governess of his choosing would follow his instructions and ignore mine. The children would be* trapped in the middle of the mistake I had made.

For myself, he would see that I became no more than an ornament at his table. If I defied him, I would pay the price. I have no doubt that he meant to punish me for questioning his authority in front of our children. Whether it would be physical or emotional, I didn't know, but I was sure the damage would be severe. Discontent I might hide from the children, open animosity I could not.

I would take them and go, find somewhere we could disappear. But first I went to Christian.

The night was moon-washed and breezy. I kept my cloak pulled tight, the hood over my hair. The puppy was snuggled at my breast. I had the carriage take me to the village, then walked to his cottage through the quiet streets with the smell of water and flowers all around. My heart was pounding in my ears as I knocked. This was the first step, and once taken, I could never go back.

But it wasn't fear, no, it wasn't fear that trembled through me when he opened the door. It was relief. The moment I saw him I knew the choice had already been made.

"Bianca," he said. "What are you thinking of?"

"I must talk to you." He was already pulling me inside. I saw that he'd been reading in the lamplight. Its warm glow and the scent of his paints soothed me more than words. I set the pup down and he immediately began to explore, sniffing into corners and making himself at home.

Christian made me sit, and no doubt sensing my nerves, brought me a brandy. As I sipped, I told him of the scene with Fergus. Though I struggled to remain calm, I could see his face, the violence in it, as his hands had closed over my throat.

"My God!" With this, Christian was crouching beside my chair, his fingers skimming up my throat. I hadn't known there were bruises there where Fergus's thumbs had pressed.

Christian's eyes went black. His hands gripped the arms of the chair before he lunged to his feet. "I'll kill him for this."

I jumped up to stop him from storming out of the cottage. My fear was such I'm not sure what I said, though I know I told him that Fergus had left for Boston, that I couldn't bear more violence. In the end it was my tears that stopped him. He held me as though I was a child, rocking and comforting while I poured out my heart and my desperation.

Perhaps I should have been ashamed to have begged him to take me and the children away, to have thrust that kind of burden and responsibility on him. If he had refused, I know I would have gone on alone, taken my three babies to some quiet village in Ireland or England. But Christian wiped away my tears.

"Of course we'll go. I'll not see you or the children spend another night under the same roof with him. He'll never lay a hand on any of you again. It will be difficult, Bianca. You and the children won't have the kind of life you're used to. And the scandal —"

"I don't care about the scandal. The children need to feel loved and safe." I rose then, to pace. "I can't be sure what's right. Night after night I've lain in bed asking myself if I have the right to love you, to want you. I took vows, made promises, and was given three children." I covered my face with my hands. "A part of me will always suffer for breaking those vows, but I must do something. I think I'll go mad if I don't. God may never forgive me, but I can't face a lifetime of unhappiness."

He took my hands to pull them away from my face. "We were meant to be to-gether. We knew it, both of us, the first time we saw each other. I was content with those few hours as long as I knew you were safe. But I'll not stand by and see you give your life to a man who'll abuse you. From tonight, you're mine, and will be mine forever. Nothing and no one will change that."

I believed him. With his face close to mine, his fine gray eyes so clear and sure, I believed. And I needed.

"Then tonight, make me yours."

I felt like a bride. The moment he touched me, I knew I had never been touched before. His eyes were on mine as he took the pins from my hair. His fingers trembled. Nothing, nothing has ever moved me more than knowing I had the power to weaken him. His lips were gentle against mine even as I felt the ten-sion vibrating through his body. There in the lamplight he unfastened my dress, and I his shirt. And a bird began to sing in the brush.

I could see by the way he looked at me that I pleased him. Slowly, almost torturously he drew off my petticoats, my corset. Then he touched my hair, running his hands through it, and looking his fill.

"I'll paint you like this one day," he murmured. "For myself."

He lifted me into his arms, and I could feel his heart pounding in his chest as he carried me to the bedroom.

The light was silver, the air like wine. This was no hurried coupling in the dark, but a dance as graceful as a waltz, and as exhilarating. No matter how impossible it seems, it was as though we had loved countless times before, as though I had felt that hard, firm body against mine night after night.

This was a world I had never experienced, yet it was achingly, beautifully familiar. Each movement, each sigh, each need was as natural as breath. Even when the urgency stunned me, the beauty didn't lessen. As he made me his, I knew I had found something every soul searches for. Simple love.

Leaving him was the most difficult thing I have ever done. Though we told each other it would be the last time we were separated, we lingered and loved again. It was nearly dawn before I returned to The Towers. When I looked at the house, walked through it, I knew I would miss it desperately. This, more than any place in my life, had been home. Christian and I, with the children, would make our own, but I would always hold The Towers in my heart.

There was little I would take with me. In the quiet before sunrise, I packed a small case. Nanny would help me put together what the children would need, but this I wanted to do alone. Perhaps it was a symbol of independence. And perhaps that is why I thought of the emeralds. They were the only things Fergus had given me that I considered mine. There were times I had detested them, knowing they had been given to me as a prize for producing a proper heir.

Yet they were mine, as my children were mine.

I didn't think of their monetary value as I took them out, held them in my hands and watched them gleam in the light of the lamp. They would be a legacy for my children, and their children, a symbol of freedom, and of hope. And with Christian, of love.

As dawn broke, I decided to put them, together with this journal, in a safe place until I joined Christian again.

# Chapter Ten

The woman seemed ancient. She sat, looking as frail and brittle as old glass, in the shade of a gnarled elm. Close by, pert young pansies basked in a square of sunlight and flirted with droning bees. Residents made use of the winding stone paths through the lawns of the Madison House. Some were wheeled by family or attendants; others walked, in pairs or alone, with the careful hesitance of age.

There were birds trilling. The woman listened, nodding to herself as she plied a crochet hook and thread with fingers that refused to surrender to arthritis. She wore bright pink slacks and a cotton blouse that had been a gift from one of her great-grandchildren. She had always loved vivid colors. Some things don't fade with age.

Her skin was nut-brown, as creased and lined as an old map. Until two years before, she had lived on her own, tending her own garden, cooking her own meals. But a fall, a bad one that had left her helpless with pain on her kitchen floor for nearly twelve hours, had convinced her it was time to change.

Stubborn and set in her ways, she had refused offers by several members of her large family to live with them. If she couldn't have her own place, she'd be damned if she would be a burden. She'd been comfortably off, well able to afford a good home and good medical care. At the Madison House, she had her own room. And if the days of puttering in her garden were past, at least she could enjoy the flowers here.

She had company if she wanted it, privacy if she didn't. Millie Tobias figured that at ninety-eight and counting, she'd earned the right to choose.

She was pleased that she was having visitors. Yes, she thought as she worked her needle, she was right pleased. The day had already started off well. She'd awakened that morning with no more than the usual sundry aches. Her hip was twitching a bit, which meant rain on the way. No matter, she mused. It was good for the flowers.

Her hands worked, but she rarely glanced at them. They knew what to do with needle and thread. Instead, she watched the path, her eyes aided by thick, tinted lenses. She saw the young couple, the lanky young man with shaggy dark hair; the willowy girl in a thin summer dress, her hair the color of October leaves. They walked close, hand in hand. Millie had a soft spot for young lovers and decided they looked pretty as a picture.

Her fingers kept moving as they walked off the path to join her in the shade.

"Mrs. Tobias?"

She studied Max, saw earnest blue eyes and a shy smile. "Ayah," she said. "And you'd be Dr. Quartermain." Her voice was a crackle, heavy with down-east. "Making doctors young these days."

"Yes, ma'am. This is Lilah Calhoun."

Not a shy bone in this one, Millie decided, and wasn't displeased when Lilah sat on the grass at her feet to admire the crocheting.

"This is beautiful." Lilah touched a fingertip to the gossamer blue thread. "What will it be?"

"What it wants to. You're from the island."

"Yes, I was born there."

Millie let out a little sigh. "Haven't been back in thirty years. Couldn't bear to live there after I lost my Tom, but I still miss the sound of the sea."

"You were married a long time?"

"Fifty years. We had a good life. We made eight children, and saw all of them grown. Now I've got twenty-three grand-children, fifteen great-grandchildren and seven great-great-grandchildren." She let out a wheezy laugh. "Sometimes I feel like I've propagated this old world all on my own. Take your hands out of your pockets, boy," she said to Max. "And come on down here so's I don't have to crane my neck." She waited until he was settled. "This here your sweetheart?" she asked him.

"Ah . . . well . . ."

"Well, is she or isn't she?" Millie de-manded, and flashed her dentures in a grin.

"Yes, Max." Lilah sent him an amused and lazy smile. "Is she or isn't she?"

Cornered, Max let out a little huff of breath. "I suppose you could say so."

"Slow to make up his mind, is he?" she said to Lilah and winked. "Nothing wrong with that. You've got the look of her," she said abruptly.

"Of whom?"

"Bianca Calhoun. Isn't that what you came to talk to me about?"

Lilah laid a hand on Millie's arm. The flesh was thin as paper. "You remember her."

"Ayah. She was a great lady. Beautiful with a good and kind heart. Doted on her children. A lot of the wealthy ladies who came summering on the island were happy to leave their children to nursemaids and nannies, but Mrs. Calhoun liked to see to them herself. She was always taking them for walks, or spending time in the nursery. Saw them off to bed herself, every night, unless her husband made plans that would take her out before their bedtime. A good mother she was, and nothing better can be said of a woman than that."

She gave a decisive nod and perked up when she saw that Max was taking notes. "I worked there three summers, 1912, '13 and '14." And with the odd trick of old age, she could remember them with perfect clarity.

"Do you mind?" Max took out a small tape recorder. "It would help us remember everything you tell us."

"Don't mind a bit." In fact, it pleased her enormously. She thought it was just like being on a TV talk show. Her fingers worked away as she settled more comfortably in the chair. "You live in The Towers still?" she asked Lilah.

"Yes, my family and I."

"How many times I climbed up and down those stairs. The master, he didn't like us using the main staircase, but when he wasn't about, I used to come down that way and fancy myself a lady. A-swishing my skirts and holding my nose in the air. Oh, I was a pistol in those days, and not hard to look at either. Used to flirt with one of the gardeners. Joseph was his name. But that was just to make my Tom jealous, and hurry him along a bit."

She sighed, looking back. "Never seen a house like it, before or since. The furniture, the paintings, the crystal. Once a week we'd wash every window with vinegar so they'd sparkle like diamonds. And the mistress, she'd like fresh flowers everywhere. She'd cut roses and peonies out of the garden, or pick the wild orchids and lady's slippers."

"What can you tell us about the summer she died?" Max prompted.

"She spent a lot of time in her tower room that summer, looking out the window at the cliffs, or writing in her book."

"Book?" Lilah interrupted. "Do you mean a journal, a diary?"

"I suppose that's what it was. I saw her writing in it sometimes when I brought her up some tea. She'd always thank me, too. Call me by name. 'Thank you, Millie,' she would say, 'it's a pretty day.' Or, 'You didn't have to trouble, Millie. How is your young man?' Gracious, she was." Millie's mouth thinned. "Now the master, he wouldn't say a word to you. Might as well have been a stick of wood for all he noticed."

"You didn't like him," Max put in.

"Wasn't my place to like or dislike, but a harder, colder man I've never met in all my years. We'd talk about it sometimes, me and one of the other girls. Why did such a sweet and lovely woman marry a man like that? Money, I would have said. Oh, the clothes she had, and the parties, the jewelry. But it didn't make her happy. Her eyes were sad. She and the master would go out in the evenings, or they'd entertain at home. He'd go his own way most other times, business and politics and the like, hardly paying any mind to his wife, and less to his children. Though he was partial to the boy, the oldest boy."

"Ethan," Lilah supplied. "My grandfather."

"A fine little boy, he was, and a handful.

He liked to slide down the banisters and play in the dirt. The mistress didn't mind him getting dirty, but she made certain he was all polished up when the master got home. A tight ship he ran, Fergus Calhoun. Was it any wonder the poor woman looked elsewhere for a little softness?"

Lilah closed a hand over Max's. "You knew she was seeing someone?"

"It was my job to clean the tower room. More than once I looked out that window and saw her running out to the cliffs. She met a man there. I know she was a married woman, but it wasn't for me to judge then, or now. Whenever she came back from seeing him, she looked happy. At least for a little while."

"Do you know who he was?" Max asked her.

"No. A painter, I think, because there were times he had an easel set up. But I never asked anyone, and never told what I saw. It was the mistress's secret. She deserved one."

Because her hands were tiring, she let them still in her lap. "The day before she died, she brought a little puppy home for the children. A stray she said she'd found out on the cliffs. Lord, what a commotion.

The children were wild about that dog. The mistress had one of the gardeners fill up a tub on the patio, and she and the children washed the pup themselves. They were laughing, the dog was howling. The mistress ruined one of her pretty day frocks. After, I helped the nanny clean up the children. It was the last time I saw them happy."

She paused a moment to gather her thoughts while two butterflies danced toward the pansies. "There was a dreadful fight when the master came home. I'd never heard the mistress raise her voice before. They were in the parlor and I was in the hall. I could hear them plain. The master wouldn't have the dog in the house. Of course, the children were crying, but he said, just as cold, that the mistress was to give it to one of the servants and have it destroyed."

Lilah felt her own eyes fill. "But why?"

"It wasn't good enough, you see, being a mutt. The little girl, she stood right up to him, but she was only a wee thing, and it made no difference to him. I thought he might strike her — his voice had that meanness in it — but the mistress told the children to take the dog and go up to their nanny. It got worse after that. The mistress was fit to be tied. I wouldn't have said she had a temper, but she cut loose. The master said terrible things to her, vicious things. He said he was going to Boston for a few days, and that she was to get rid of the dog, and to remember her place. When he came out of the parlor, his face — I'll never forget it. He looked mad, I said to myself, then I peeked into the parlor and there was the mistress, white as a ghost, just sitting in a chair with her hand pressed to her throat. The next night, she was dead."

Max said nothing for a moment. Lilah was looking away, her eyes blind with tears. "Mrs. Tobias, had you heard anything about Bianca planning to leave her husband?"

"Later I did. The master, he dismissed the nanny, even though those poor babies were wild with grief. She — Mary Beals was her name — she loved the children and the mistress like they were her own. I saw her in the village the day they were to take the mistress back to New York for burying. She told me that her lady would never have killed herself, that she would never have done that to the children. She insisted that it had been an accident. And then she told me that the mistress had decided to leave, that she'd come to see she couldn't stay with the master. She was going to take the children away. Mary Beals said she was going to New York herself and that she was going to stay with the children no matter what Mr. Calhoun said. I heard later that she'd gotten her position back."

"Did you ever see the Calhoun emeralds, Mrs. Tobias?" Max asked.

"Oh, ayah. Once seen, you'd never forget them. She would wear them and look like a queen. They disappeared the night she died." A faint smile moved her mouth. "I know the legend, boy. You could say I lived it."

Composed again, Lilah looked back. "Do you have any idea what happened to them?"

"I know Fergus Calhoun never threw them into the sea. He wouldn't so much as flip a penny into a wishing well, so close with his money he was. If she meant to leave him, then she meant to take them with her. But he came back, you see."

Max's brows drew together. "Came back?"

"The master came back the afternoon of the day she died. That's why she hid them. And the poor thing never had a chance to take them, and her children, and get away."

"Where?" Lilah murmured. "Where could she have put them?"

"In that house, who could say?" Millie picked up her work again. "I went back to help pack up her things. A sad day. Wasn't one of us dry-eyed. We put all her lovely dresses in tissue paper and locked them in a trunk. We were told to clear the room out, even her hair combs and perfume. He wanted nothing left of her in there. I never saw the emeralds again."

"Or her journal?" Max waited while Millie pursed her lips. "Did you find the journal in her room?"

"No." Slowly she shook her head. "There was no diary."

"How about stationery, or cards, letters?"

"Her writing paper was in the desk, and the little book she kept her appointments in, but I didn't see a diary. We put everything away, didn't even leave a hairpin. The next summer, he came back. He kept her room locked up, and there wasn't a sign of the mistress in the house. There had been photographs, and a painting, but they were gone. The children hardly laughed. Once I came across the little boy standing outside his mother's room, just staring at the door. I gave my notice in the middle of the season. I couldn't bear to work in that house, not with the master. He'd grown even colder, harder. And he took to going up to the tower room and sitting for hours. I married Tom that summer, and never went back to The Towers."

Later Lilah stood on the narrow balcony of their hotel room. Below she could see the long blue rectangle of the pool, hear the laughter and splashing of families and couples enjoying their vacation.

But her mind wasn't on the bright summer sun or the shouts and rippling water. It was on the days eighty years past, when women wore long, graceful dresses and wrote their dreams in private journals.

When Max came up quietly behind her to slip his arms around her waist, she leaned back into him, comforted.

"I always knew she was unhappy," Lilah said. "I could feel that. Just as I could feel she was hopelessly in love. But I never knew she was afraid. I never picked up on that."

"It was a long time ago, Lilah." Max pressed a kiss to her hair. "Mrs. Tobias might have exaggerated. Remember, she was a young, impressionable woman when it all happened."

Lilah turned to look quietly, deeply into his eyes. "You don't believe that."

"No." He stroked his knuckles over her cheek. "But we can't change what happened. We can't help her now."

"But we can, don't you see? By finding the necklace, and the journal. She must have written everything she felt in that book. Everything she wanted, and feared. She wouldn't have left it where Fergus would find it. If she hid the emeralds, she hid the book, too."

"Then we'll find them. If we follow Mrs. Tobias's account, Fergus came back before Bianca expected him. She didn't have the opportunity to get the emeralds out of the house. They're still there, so it's only a matter of time before we find them."

"But —"

He shook his head, cupping his hands around her face. "Aren't you the one who says to trust your feelings? Think about it. Trent comes to The Towers and falls in love with C.C. Because of his idea to renovate and turn part of the house into a retreat, the old legend comes out. Once it's made public, Livingston or Caufield or whatever we choose to call him develops an obsession. He makes a play for Amanda, but she's already hooked on

Sloan — who's also there because of the house. Caufield's impatient, so he steals some of the papers. That brings me into it. You fish me out of the water, take me into your home. Since then we've been able to piece more together. We've found a photograph of the emeralds. We've located a woman who actually knew Bianca, and who's corroborated the fact that she hid the necklace in the house. It's all connected, every step. Do you think we'd have gotten this far if we weren't meant to find them?"

Her eyes softened as she linked her hands over his wrists. "You're awfully good for me, Professor. A little optimistic logic's just what I need right now."

"Then I'll give you some more. I think the next step is to start tracking down the artist."

"Christian? But how?"

"You leave it to me."

"All right." Wanting his arms around her, she laid her head on his shoulder. "There's another connection. You might think it's out of left field, but I can't help thinking about it."

"Tell me."

"A couple of months ago, Trent was walking the cliffs. He found Fred. We've

266

never been able to figure out what the puppy was doing out there all alone. It made me think of the little dog Bianca brought to her children, the one she and Fergus argued about so bitterly only a day before she died. I wonder what happened to that dog, Max." She let out a long sigh. "Then I think about those children. It's difficult to imagine one's grandfather as a little boy. I never even knew him because he died before I was born. But I can see him, standing outside of his mother's door, grieving. And it breaks my heart."

"Shh." He tightened his arms around her. "It's better to think that Bianca had some happiness with her artist. Can't you see her running to him on the cliffs, stealing a few hours in the sun, or finding some quiet place where they could be alone?"

"Yes." Her lips curved against his throat. "Yes, I can. Maybe that's why I love sitting in the tower. She wasn't always unhappy there, not when she thought of him."

"And if there's any justice, they're together now."

Lilah tilted her head back to look at him. "Yes, you are awfully good for me. Tell you what, why don't we take advantage of that pool down there? I'd like to swim with you when it wasn't a matter of life or death."

He kissed her forehead. "You've got a deal."

She did more floating than swimming. Max had never seen anyone who could actually sleep on the water. But Lilah could — her eyes comfortably closed behind tinted glasses, her body totally relaxed. She wore two tiny scraps of leopard-print cloth that raised Max's blood pressure — and that of every other male within a hundred yards. But she drifted, hands moving gently in the water. Occasionally she would kick into a lazy sidestroke, her hair flowing out around her. Now and again, she would reach out to link her hand with his, or twine her arms around his neck, trusting him to keep her buoyant.

Then she kissed him, her lips wet and cool, her body as fluid as the water around them.

"Time for a nap," she said, and left him in the pool to stretch out on a chaise under an umbrella.

When she awoke, the shadows were long and only a few diehards were left in the water. She looked around for Max, vaguely disappointed that he hadn't stayed with her. Gathering up her wrap, she went back inside to find him.

The room was empty, but there was a note on the bed in his careful handwriting.

*Had a couple of things to see to. Be back soon.*

With a shrug, she tuned the radio to a classical station and went in to take a long, steamy shower.

Revived and relaxed, she toweled off, then began to cream her skin in long, lazy strokes. Maybe they could find some cozy little restaurant for dinner, she mused. Someplace where there were dim corners and music. They could linger over the meal while the candles burned down, and drink cool, sparkling wine.

Then they would come back, draw the drapes on the balcony, close themselves in. He would kiss her in that thorough, drugging way until they couldn't keep their hands off each other. She picked up her bottle of scent, spritzing it onto her softened skin. They would make love slowly or frantically, gently or desperately, until, tangled together, they slept.

They wouldn't think about Bianca or tragedies, about emeralds or thieves. Tonight they would only think about each other.

Dreaming of him, she stepped out into the bedroom.

He was waiting for her. It seemed he'd been waiting for her all of his life. She paused, her eyes darkened by the candles he'd lit, her damp hair gleaming with the delicate light. Her scent wafted into the room, mysterious, seductive, to tangle with the fragrance of the clutch of freesias he'd bought her.

Like her, he had imagined a perfect night and had tried to bring it to her.

The radio still played, low romantic strings. On the table in front of the open balcony doors two slender white tapers glowed. Champagne, just poured, frothed in tall tulip glasses. Behind the table, the sun was sinking in the sky, a scarlet ball, bleeding into the deepening blue.

"I thought we'd eat in," he said, and held out a hand for hers.

"Max." Emotion tightened her throat. "I was right all along." Her fingers linked with his. "You are a poet."

"I want to be alone with you." Taking one of the fragile blooms, he slipped it into her hair. "I'd hoped you wouldn't mind."

"No." She let out a shaky breath when he pressed his lips to her palm. "I don't mind."

He picked up the glasses, handed her one. "Restaurants are so crowded."

"And noisy," she agreed, touching her glass to his.

"And someone might object if I nibbled on you rather than the appetizers."

Watching him, she took a sip. "I wouldn't."

He slid a finger up her throat, then tilted her chin so that their lips met. "We'd better give dinner a try," he said after a long moment.

They sat, close together to watch the sun set, to feed each other little bites of lobster drenched with sweet, melted butter. She let champagne explode on her tongue, then turned her mouth to his where the flavor was just as intoxicating.

As a Chopin prelude drifted from the radio, he pressed a light kiss to her shoulder, then skimmed more up her throat.

"The first time I saw you," he said as he slipped a bite of lobster between her lips, "I thought you were a mermaid. And I dreamed about you that first night." Gently he rubbed his lips over hers. "I've dreamed about you every night since."

"When I sit up in the tower, I think about you — the way I imagine Bianca once thought about Christian. Do you think they ever made love?"

"He couldn't have resisted her."

Her breath shuddered out between her lips. "She wouldn't have wanted him to." With her eyes on his, she began to unbutton his shirt. "She would have ached needing him, wanting to touch him." On a sigh, she ran her hands over his chest. "When they were together, alone together, nothing else could have mattered."

"He would have been half-mad for her." Taking her hands, he brought her to her feet. He left her for a moment, to draw the shades so that they were closed in with music and candlelight. "Thoughts of her would have haunted him, day and night. Her face . . ." He skimmed his fingers over Lilah's cheeks, over her jaw, down her throat. "Every time he closed his eyes, he would have seen it. Her taste . . ." He pressed his lips to hers. "Every time he took a breath it would be there to remind him what it was like to kiss her."

"And she would have lain in bed, night after night, wanting his touch." Heart racing, she pushed the shirt from his shoulders, then shivered when he reached for the belt of her robe. "Remembering how he looked at her when he undressed her."

"He couldn't have wanted her more than I want you." The robe slithered to the floor. His arms drew her closer. "Let me show you."

The candles burned low. A single thread of moonlight slashed through the chink in the drapes. There was music, swelling with passion, and the scent of fragile flowers.

Murmured promises. Desperate answers. A low husky laugh, a sobbing gasp. From patience to urgency, from tenderness to madness, they drove each other. Through the dark, endless night they were tireless and greedy. A gentle touch could cause a tremor; a rough caress a soft sigh. They came together with generous affection, then again like warriors.

Each time they thought they were sated, they would turn to each other once more to arouse or to soothe, to cling or to stroke, until the candles gutted out and the gray light of dawn crept into the room.

# Chapter Eleven

Hawkins was sick and tired of waiting around. As far as he was concerned every day on the island was a day wasted. Worse, he'd given up a tidy little job in New York that would have earned him at least ten grand. Instead, he'd invested half that much in a heist that looked more and more like a bust.

He knew Caufield was good. The fact was, there were few better at lifting locks and dancing around the police. In the ten years of their association, they had pulled off some very smooth operations. Which was why he was worried.

There was nothing smooth about this job. Damn college boy had messed things up good and proper. Hawkins resented the fact that Caufield wouldn't let him take care of Quartermain. He knew Caufield didn't think he had any finesse, but he could have arranged a nice, quiet accident.

The real problem was that Caufield was obsessed with the emeralds. He talked about them day and night — and he talked as though they were living things rather than some pretty sparklers that would bring in some good, crisp cash.

Hawkins was beginning to believe that Caufield didn't intend to fence the emeralds after all. He smelled the double cross and had been watching his partner like a hawk. Every time Caufield went out, Hawkins would pace the empty house, looking for some clue to his partner's true intentions.

Then there were the rages. Caufield was well-known for his unstable temper, but those ugly tantrums were becoming more frequent. The day before, he had stormed into the house, white-faced and wild-eyed, his body trembling with fury because the Calhoun woman hadn't been at her station in the park. He'd trashed one of the rooms, hacking away at furniture with a kitchen knife until he'd come to himself again.

Hawkins was afraid of him. Though he was a stocky man with ready fists, he had no desire to match Caufield physically. Not when the man got that gleam in his eyes.

His only hope now, if he wanted his rightful share and a clean escape, was to outwit his partner.

With Caufield out of the house again, haunting the park, Hawkins began a slow, methodical search. Though he was a big man, often considered dull witted by his associates, he could toss a room and hardly raise the dust. He sifted through the stolen papers, then turned away in disgust. There was nothing of use there. If Caufield had found anything, he would never have left it in plain view. He decided to start with the obvious, his partner's bedroom.

He shook out the books first. He knew Caufield liked to pretend he was educated, even erudite, though he'd had no more schooling than Hawkins himself. There was nothing in the volumes of Shakespeare and Steinbeck but words.

Hawkins searched under the mattress, through the drawers in the bureau. Since Caufield's pistol wasn't around, he decided the man had tucked it into his knapsack before setting off to find Lilah. Patient, Hawkins looked behind the mirrors, behind drawers, beneath the rug. He was beginning to think he had misjudged his partner when he turned to the closet.

There, in the pocket of a pair of jeans, he found the map.

It was crudely drawn on yellowed paper. For Hawkins, there was no mistaking its meaning. The Towers was clearly depicted, along with direction and distance and a few out-of-proportion landmarks.

The map to the emeralds, Hawkins thought as he smoothed out the creases. A bitter fury filled him while he studied each line and marker. The double-dealing Caufield had found it among the stolen papers and hidden it away for himself. Well, two could play that game, he thought. He slipped out of the room as he tucked the paper into his own pocket. Wouldn't Caufield have a fine rage when he discovered his partner had snatched the emeralds out from under his nose. Hawkins thought it was almost a pity that he wouldn't be around to see it.

He found Christian. It was so much easier than Max had supposed that he could only sit and stare at the book in his hand. In less than a half day in the library, he'd stumbled across the name in a dusty volume titled *Artists and Their Art: 1900– 1950*. He had patiently dug away through the As, was meticulously slogging through the Bs, when there it was. Christian Bradford, 1884– 1976. Though the given name had caused Max to perk up, he hadn't expected it to be so easy. But it all fell into place.

*Though Bradford did not come to enjoy any real success until his last years, his early work has become valuable since his death.*

Max skimmed over the treatise on the artist's style.

*Considered a gypsy in his day, due to his habit of moving from one location to another, Bradford often sold his work for room and board. A prolific artist, he would often complete a painting in a matter of days. It is said he would work for twenty hours straight when the mood was on him. It remains a mystery why he produced nothing during the years between 1914 and 1916.*

Oh God, Max thought, and rubbed his damp palms on his slacks.

*Married in 1925 to Margaret Doogan, Bradford had one child, a son. Little more is known about his personal life, as he remained an obsessively private man until his death. He suffered a debilitating heart attack in the late sixties, but continued to paint. He died in Bar Harbor, Maine, where he had kept a cottage for more than a half century. He was survived by his son and a grandson.*

"I've found you," Max murmured. Turning the page, he studied the reproduction of one of Bradford's works. It was a storm, fighting its way in from the sea. Passionate, violent, frenzied. It was a view Max knew — the view from the cliffs beneath The Towers.

An hour later, a half-dozen books under his arm, he arrived home. There was still an hour before he could pick up Lilah at the park, an hour before he could tell her they had jumped the next hurdle. Giddy with success, he greeted Fred so exuberantly that the dog raced up and down the hall, running into walls and tripping on his tail.

"Goodness." Coco trotted down the stairs. "What a commotion."

"Sorry."

"No need to apologize, I wouldn't know what to do if a day went by without a commotion. Why, Max, you look positively delighted with yourself."

"Well, as it happens, I —"

He broke off when Alex and Jenny came bounding down, firing invisible laser pistols. "Dead meat!" Alex shouted. "Dead meat!"

"If you must kill something," Coco said,

"please do it outside. Fred needs an airing anyway."

"Death to the invaders," Alex announced. "We'll fry them like bacon."

In total agreement, Jenny aimed her laser at Fred and sent the dog scampering down the hall again. Deciding he made a handy invader, they raced after him. Even with the distance, the sound of the back door slamming boomed through the house.

"I don't know where they get those violent imaginations," Coco commented with a relieved sigh. "Suzanna's so mild tempered, and their father . . ." Something dark came into her eyes when she trailed off. "Well, that's another story. So tell me, what has you so happy?"

"I was just in the library, and I —"

This time it was the phone that interrupted. Coco slipped off an earring as she picked up the receiver. "Hello. Yes. Oh, yes, he's right here." She cupped a hand over the mouthpiece. "It's your dean, dear. He'd like to speak to you."

Max set the books on the telephone stand as Coco began to straighten pictures a few discreet feet away. "Dean Hodgins? Yes, I am, thank you. It's a beautiful spot. Well, I haven't really decided when I'm coming back . . . Professor Blake?"

Coco glanced back at the alarm in his voice.

"When? Is it serious? I'm sorry he's ill. I hope . . . I beg your pardon?" Letting out a long breath, Max leaned back against the banister. "I'm very flattered, but —" He lapsed into silence again, dragging a hand through his hair. "Thank you. Yes, I understand that. If I could have a day or two to consider. I appreciate it. Yes, sir. Goodbye."

When he simply stood, staring into space, Coco cleared her throat. "I hope it wasn't bad news, dear."

"What?" He focused on her, then shook his head. "No, well, yes. That is, the head of the history department had a heart attack last week."

"Oh." Immediately sympathetic, Coco came forward. "How dreadful."

"It was mild — if you can term anything like that mild. The doctors consider it a warning. They're recommending that he cut back on his work load, and he's taken them seriously, because he's decided to retire." He gave Coco a baffled look. "It seems he's recommended me to take over his position."

"Well now." She smiled and patted his cheek, but she was watching him carefully. "That's quite an honor, isn't it?"

281

"I'd have to go back next week," he said to himself. "To take over as acting head of the department until a final decision's made."

"Sometimes it's difficult to know what to do, which fork in the road to take. Why don't we have a nice cup of tea?" she suggested. "Then I'll read the leaves and we'll see."

"I really don't think —" The next interruption relieved him, and Coco clucked her tongue as she went to answer the banging on the door.

"Oh, my" was all she said. With her hand pressed to her breast, she said it again. "Oh, my!"

"Don't just stand there with your mouth hanging open, Cordelia," a crisp, authoritative voice demanded. "Have someone deal with my bags."

"Aunt Colleen." Coco's hand fluttered to her side. "What a . . . lovely surprise."

"Ha! You'd as soon see Satan himself on the doorstep." Leaning on a glossy, gold-tipped cane, she marched across the threshold.

Max saw a tall, rail-thin woman with a mass of luxurious white hair. She wore an elegant white suit and gleaming pearls. Her skin, generously lined, was as pale as linen. She might have been a ghost but for the deep blue eyes that scanned him.

"Who the hell is this?"

"Um. Um."

"Speak up, girl. Don't stutter." Colleen tapped the cane impatiently. "You never kept a lick of the sense God gave you."

Coco began to wring her hands. "Aunt Colleen, this is Dr. Quartermain. Max, Colleen Calhoun."

"Doctor," Colleen barked. "Who's sick? Damned if I'm going to stay in a contagious house."

"That's a Ph.D., Miss Calhoun." Max offered a cautious smile. "It's nice to meet you."

"Ha." She sniffed and glanced around the hall. "Still letting the place fall down around your ears. Best if it was struck by lightning. Burned to the ground. See to those bags, Cordelia, and have someone bring me some tea. I've had a long trip." So saying, she clumped off toward the parlor.

"Yes, ma'am." Hands still fluttering, Coco sent Max a helpless look. "I hate to ask . . ."

"Don't worry about it. Where should I take her luggage?"

"Oh, God." Coco pressed her hands to her cheeks. "The first room on the right on the second floor. We'll have to stall her so that I can prepare it. Oh, and she won't have paid the driver. Tightfisted old . . . I'll call Amanda. She can warn the others. Max —" she clutched his hands "— if you believe in prayer, use it now and pray that this is a very short visit."

"Where's the damn tea?" Colleen demanded in a bellow and thumped her cane.

"Just coming." Coco turned and raced down the hall.

Pulling all her rabbits out of her hat, Coco plied her aunt with tea and petits fours, dragged Trent and Sloan away from their work and begged Max to fall in. Arrangements were made for Amanda to pick up Lilah and for Suzanna to close early and pitch in to prepare the guest room.

It was like preparing for an invasion, Max thought as he joined the group in the parlor. Colleen sat, erect as a general, while she measured her opponents with the same steely eye.

"So, you're the one who married Catherine. Hotels, isn't it?"

"Yes, ma'am," Trent answered politely while Coco fluttered around the room.

284

"Never stay in 'em," Colleen said dismissively. "Got married quick, wouldn't you say?"

"I didn't want to give her a chance to change her mind."

She almost smiled, then sniffed and aimed at Sloan. "And you're the one who's after Amanda."

"That's right."

"What's that accent?" she demanded, eyes sharpening. "Where are you from?"

"Oklahoma."

"O'Riley," she mused for a moment, then pointed a long white finger. "Oil."

"There you go."

"Humph." She lifted her tea to sip. "So you've got some harebrained notion about turning the west wing into a hotel. Better off burning it down and claiming the insurance."

"Aunt Colleen." Scandalized, Coco gaped at her. "You don't mean that."

"I say what I mean. Hated this place most of my life." She shifted to brood up at the portrait of her father. "He'd have hated seeing paying guests in The Towers. It would have mortified him."

"I'm sorry, Aunt Colleen," Coco began. "But we have to make the best of things."

"Did I ask for an apology?" Colleen

snapped. "Where the hell are my grand-nieces? Don't they have the courtesy to pay their respects?"

"They'll be along soon." Desperate, Coco poured more tea. "This was so unexpected, and we've —"

"A home should always be prepared for guests," Colleen retaliated with relish, then frowned at the doorway when Suzanna came in. "Which one is this?"

"I'm Suzanna." Dutifully she came forward to kiss her great-aunt's cheek.

"You favor your mother," Colleen decided with a grudging nod. "I was fond of Deliah." She shot a look at Max. "You after her?"

He blinked as Sloan struggled to turn a laugh into a cough. "Ah, no. No, ma'am."

"Why not? Something wrong with your eyes?"

"No." He shifted in his chair as Suzanna grinned and settled on a hassock.

"Max is visiting for a few weeks," said Coco, coming to the rescue. "He's helping us out with a little — historical research."

"The emeralds." Eyes gleaming, Colleen sat back. "Don't take me for a fool, Cordelia. We get newspapers aboard ship. Cruise ships," she said to Trent. "Much more civilized than hotels. Now, tell me what the hell is going on around here."

"Nothing, really." Coco cleared her throat again. "You know how the press blows things out of proportion."

"Was there a thief in this house, shooting off a gun?"

"Well, yes. It was disturbing, but —"

"You." Colleen hefted her cane and poked it at Max. "You with the Ph.D. I assume you can articulate clearly. Explain the situation, briefly."

At the pleading glance from Coco, Max set his unwanted tea aside. "The family decided, after a series of events, to investigate the veracity of the legend of the Calhoun emeralds. Unfortunately, news of the necklace leaked, causing interest and speculation among various people, some of them unsavory. The first step was to catalogue old family papers, to verify the existence of the emeralds."

"Of course they existed," Colleen said impatiently. "Haven't I seen them with my own eyes?"

"You were difficult to reach," Coco began, and was silenced with a look.

"In any case," Max continued. "The house was broken into, and a number of the papers stolen." Max skimmed over his involvement to bring her up to date.

"Hmm." Colleen frowned at him. "What do you do, write?"

Max's brow lifted in surprise. "I teach. History. At, ah, Cornell University."

Colleen sniffed again. "Well, you've made a mess of it. The lot of you. Bringing thieves under the roof, splashing our name all over the press, nearly getting yourselves killed. For all we know the old man sold the emeralds."

"He'd have kept a record," Max put in, and had Colleen studying him again.

"You're right there, Mr. Ph.D. He kept account of every penny he made, and every penny he spent." She closed her eyes a moment. "Nanny always told us she hid them away. For us." Fierce, her eyes opened again. "Fairy tales."

"I love fairy tales," Lilah said from the doorway. She stood, flanked by C.C. and Amanda.

"Come in here where I can see you."

"You first," Lilah muttered to C.C.

"Why me?"

"You're the youngest." She gave her sister a gentle shove.

"Throwing a pregnant woman to the wolves," Amanda muttered.

"You're next."

"What's that on your face?" Colleen demanded of C.C.

C.C. wiped a hand over her cheek. "Motor oil, I guess."

"What's the world coming to? You've got good bones," she decided. "You'll age well. You pregnant yet?"

Dipping her hands in her pockets, C.C. grinned. "As a matter of fact, yes. Trent and I are expecting in February."

"Good." Colleen waved her away. Steeling herself, Amanda stepped forward.

"Hello, Aunt Colleen. I'm glad you decided to come for the wedding."

"Might, might not." Lips pursed, she studied Amanda. "You know how to write a proper letter, in any case. It reached me last week, with the invitation." She was a lovely thing, Colleen thought, like her sisters. She felt a sense of pride in that, but would have bitten off her tongue before admitting it. "Any reason you couldn't marry a man from a nice Eastern family?"

"Yes. None of them annoyed me as much as Sloan."

With what might have been a laugh, Colleen waved her away.

When she focused on Lilah, her eyes burned and she had to press her lips tight to keep them from quivering. It was like looking at her mother, with all the years, and all the hurt wiped away.

"So, you're Lilah." When her voice cracked, she lowered her brows, looking so formidable that Coco trembled.

"Yes." Lilah kissed both her cheeks. "The last time I saw you I was eight, I think. And you scolded me for going barefoot."

"And just what are you doing with your life?"

"Oh, as little as possible," Lilah said blithely. "How about you?"

Colleen's lips twitched, but she rounded on Coco. "Haven't you taught these girls manners?"

"Don't blame her." Lilah sat on the floor at Max's feet. "We're incorrigible." She glanced over her shoulder, smiled at Max, then set a companionable hand on his knee.

Colleen didn't miss a trick. "So, you've got your eye on this one."

Tossing back her hair, Lilah smiled. "I certainly do. Cute, isn't he?"

"Lilah," Max muttered. "Give me a break."

"You didn't kiss me hello," she said quite clearly.

"Leave the boy alone." More amused than she would have admitted, Colleen thumped her cane. "At least he has manners." She waved a hand at the tea things. "Take this business away, Cordelia, and bring me a brandy."

"I'll get it." Lilah unfolded herself and strolled over to the liquor cabinet. She winked at Suzanna as her sister wheeled over the tea cart. "How long do you think she plans to make our lives a living hell?"

"I heard that."

Undaunted, Lilah turned with the brandy snifter. "Of course you did, Auntie. Papa always told us you had ears like a cat."

"Don't call me 'Auntie.' " She snatched the brandy. Colleen was used to deference — her personality and her money had always demanded it. Or to fear — the kind she easily instilled in Coco. But she enjoyed, tremendously, irreverence. "The trouble is your father never lifted a hand to any of you."

"No," Lilah murmured. "He didn't have to."

"No one loved him more than I," Colleen said briskly. "Now, it's time to decide what to do about this mess you've gotten yourselves into. The sooner mended, the sooner I can rejoin my cruise."

"You don't mean —" Coco caught herself and hastily rephrased. "Do you plan to stay with us until the emeralds are found?"

"I plan to stay until I'm ready to leave." Colleen aimed a look, daring disagreement.

"How lovely," Coco said between unsteady lips. "I believe I'll go in and see about dinner."

"I dine at seven-thirty. Precisely."

"Of course." Even as Coco rose, the familiar chaos could be heard racing down the hall. "Oh, dear."

Suzanna sprang to her feet. "I'll head them off." But she was a bit late as both children came barreling into the room.

"Cheat, cheat, cheat," Jenny accused, eyes brimming.

"Crybaby." But Alex was near tears himself as he gave her a brotherly shove.

"Who are these hooligans?" Colleen asked, interest perking.

"These hooligans are my children." Suzanna studied them both and saw that though she had tidied them herself less than twenty minutes before, they were both grimy and grim faced. Obviously her idea that they spend a quiet hour playing a board game had been a disaster.

Colleen swirled her brandy. "Bring them here. I'll have a look at them."

"Alex, Jenny." The warning tone worked very well. "Come meet Aunt Colleen."

"She isn't going to kiss us, is she?" Alex muttered as he dragged his feet across the room.

"I certainly will not. I don't kiss grubby little boys." She had to swallow. He looked so like her baby brother, Sean. Formally she offered a hand. "How do you do?"

"Okay." Flushing a bit, he touched the thin-boned hand.

"You're awfully old," Jenny observed.

"Quite right," Colleen agreed before Suzanna could speak. "If you're lucky, the same problem will be yours one day." She would have liked to have stroked the girl's shiny blond hair, but it would have shattered her image. "I'll expect you to refrain from shouting and clattering about while I'm in the house. Furthermore . . ." She trailed off when something brushed her leg. Glancing down, she saw Fred sniffing the carpet for crumbs. "What is that?"

"That's our dog." Seized with inspiration, Alex reached down to heft the fat puppy in his arms. "If you're mean to us, he'll bite you."

"He'll do no such thing." Suzanna put a hand on Alex's shoulder.

"He might." Alex pouted. "He doesn't like bad people. Do you, Fred?"

Colleen's skin went even whiter. "What is his name?"

"His name is Fred," Jenny said gaily. "Trent found him on the cliffs and brought him home for us." She struggled the dog away from her brother to hold him out. "And he doesn't bite. He's a good dog."

"Jenny, put him down before he —"

"No." Colleen waved Suzanna's warning aside. "Let me see him." Fred wriggled, smearing dirt on Colleen's pristine white suit as she sat him in her lap. Her hands shook as they stroked his fur. "I had a dog named Fred once." A single tear spilled over and down her pale cheek. "I only had him for a little while, but I loved him very much."

Saying nothing, Lilah groped for Max's hand and held tight.

"You can play with him, if you want," Alex told her, appalled that someone so old would cry. "He doesn't really bite."

"Of course he won't bite." Recovering, Colleen set the dog on the floor, then straightened painfully. "He knows I'd just bite him back. Isn't someone going to show me to my room, or do I have to sit here all day and half the damn night?"

"We'll take you up." Lilah tugged on Max's hand so that he rose to help her to her feet.

"Bring the brandy," Colleen said imperiously, and started out stumping with her cane.

"Delightful relatives you have, Calhoun," Sloan murmured.

"Too late to back out now, O'Riley." Amanda heaved a relieved breath. "Come on, Aunt Coco, I'll help you in the kitchen."

"Which room have you stuck me in?" Only slightly breathless, Colleen paused on the second-floor landing.

"The first one, here." Max opened the door, then stepped back.

The terrace doors had been opened to let in the breeze. The furniture had been hastily polished, a few extra pieces dragged in from storage. Fresh flowers sat atop the rosewood bureau. The wallpaper was peeling, but paintings had been culled from other rooms to hide the worst of it. A delicate lace spread had been unfolded from a cedar chest and adorned the heavy four-poster.

"It'll do," Colleen muttered, determined to fight the nostalgia. "Make sure there are fresh towels, girl. And you, Quartermain, is it? Pour me another dose of that brandy and don't be stingy."

Lilah peeked into the adjoining bath and saw all was as it should be. "Is there anything else, Auntie?"

"Mind your tone, and don't call me 'Auntie.' You can send a maid up when it's time for dinner."

Lilah stuck her tongue in her cheek. "I'm afraid it's the staff's year off."

"Unconscionable." Colleen leaned heavily on her cane. "Are you telling me you haven't even day help?"

"You know very well we've been under the financial gun for some time."

"And you'll still not get a penny from me to put into this cursed place." She walked stiffly to the open doors and looked out. God, the view, she thought. It never changed. How many times over how many years had she envisioned it? "Who has my mother's room?"

"I do," Lilah said, lifting her chin.

Very slowly, Colleen turned. "Of course, you would." Her voice had softened. "Do you know how much you favor her?"

"Yes. Max found a picture in a book."

"A picture in a book." Now the bitterness. "That's all that's left of her."

"No. No, there's much more. A part of

her is still here, will always be here."

"Don't talk nonsense. Ghosts, spirits — that's Cordelia's influence, and it's a load of hogwash. Dead's dead, girl. When you're as close to it as I am, you'll know that."

"If you'd felt her as I've felt her, you'd know differently."

Colleen closed herself in. "Shut the door behind you. I like my privacy."

Lilah waited until they were out in the hall to swear. "Rude, bad-tempered old bat." Then with a lazy shrug, she tucked her arm through Max's. "Let's go get some air. To think I'd actually felt something for her downstairs when she held Fred."

"She's not so bad, Lilah." They passed through his room and onto the terrace. "You may be just as crotchety when you're eighty-something."

"I'll never be crotchety." She closed her eyes, tossed back her hair and smiled. "I'll have a nice rocking chair set in the sun and sleep old age away." She ran a hand up his arm. "Are you ever going to kiss me hello?"

"Yes." He cupped her face and did so thoroughly. "Hello. How was your day?"

"Hot and busy." But now she felt delightfully cool and relaxed. "That teacher I told you about was back. He seems overly earnest to me. Gives me the willies."

Max's smile disappeared. "You should report him to one of the rangers."

"What, for sending off bad vibrations?" She laughed and hugged him. "No, there's just something about him that hits me wrong. He's always wearing dark glasses, as if I might see something he didn't want seen if he took them off."

"You're letting your . . ." His grip tightened. "What does he look like?"

"Nothing special. Why don't we take a nap before dinner? Aunt Colleen exhausted me."

"What," Max said very precisely, "does he look like?"

"He's about your height, trim. Somewhere around thirty, I'd guess. Wears the hiker's uniform of T-shirt and ripped jeans. He doesn't have a tan," she said, frowning suddenly. "Which is odd seeing as he said he'd been camping for a couple of weeks. Average sort of brown hair, well over the collar. A very neat beard and mustache."

"It could be him." His fingers dug in as the possibility iced through him. "My God, he's been with you."

"You think — you think it's Caufield."

The idea left her shaken so that she leaned back against the wall. "What an idiot I've been. I had the same feeling, the same feeling with this man as I did when Livingston came to take Amanda out for dinner." She ran both hands through her hair. "I must be losing my touch."

Max's eyes were dark as he stared out at the cliffs. "If he comes back, I'll be ready for him."

"Don't start playing hero." Alarmed, she grabbed his arms. "He's dangerous."

"He's not getting near you again." The complete and focused intensity was back on his face. "I'll be taking your shift with you tomorrow."

# Chapter Twelve

He never let her out of his sight. Though they had given the authorities the description, Max took no chances. By the time the day was over, he knew more about the intertidal zone than anyone could want to know. He could recognize Irish moss from rockweed — though he still grimaced at Lilah's claim that the moss made excellent ice cream.

But there hadn't been a sign of Caufield.

On the off chance that he had been speaking the truth about camping in the park, the rangers had made a quiet and thorough search but had found no trace of him.

No one had seen the bearded man watching the fruitless search through field glasses. No one had seen the rage come into his eyes when he realized his cover had been blown.

As they drove home, Lilah unwound her braid. "Feel better?" she asked Max.

"No."

She pushed her hands under her hair to let the wind catch it. "Well, you should. It was sweet of you to worry about me, though."

"It has nothing to do with sweetness."

"I think you're disappointed that you didn't get to go into hand-to-hand combat."

"Maybe I am."

"Okay." She leaned over to nip at his ear. "Want to rumble?"

"It's not a joke," he muttered. "I'm not going to feel right until he's taken care of."

Lilah snuggled back in the seat. "If he had any sense he'd give up and go away. We live in the house and we've hardly made any progress."

"That's not true. We verified the existence of the emeralds. We found a photograph of them. We located Mrs. Tobias, and have her eyewitness account of what happened the day before Bianca died. And we've identified Christian."

"We've what?" She sprang up straight. "When did we identify Christian?"

Max grimaced as he glanced over at her. "I forgot to tell you. Don't look like that. First your great-aunt invades the house and sets everyone on their ears. Then you tell me about the man in the park. I thought I had told you."

She inhaled, then exhaled deeply to keep her patience. "Why don't you tell me now?"

"It was in the library yesterday," he began, and filled her in on what he'd found.

"Christian Bradford," Lilah said, trying out the name to see how it fit. "There's something familiar about it. I wonder if I've seen some of his paintings. It wouldn't be surprising if there were some in this area, since he lived here on and off. Died here."

"Didn't you study art in college?"

"I didn't study at all unless I was boxed in. Mostly I drifted through, and art was always more a hobby than anything else. I didn't want to work at it because I liked playing at it better. And I wanted to be a naturalist all along."

"An ambition?" He grinned. "Lilah, you'll ruin your image."

"Well, it was my only one. Everybody's entitled. Bradford, Bradford," she repeated, gnawing at the word. "I'd swear it rings a bell." She closed her eyes on it, opening them again when they pulled up at The Towers. "Got it. We knew a Bradford. He grew up on the island. Holt, Holt Bradford. The dark, broody, surly sort. He was a few years older — probably in his early thirties now. He left ten or twelve years ago, but it seems to me I heard he was back. He owns a cottage in the village. My God, Max, if he's Christian's grandson, it would be the same cottage."

"Don't get ahead of yourself. We'll look into it, one step at a time."

"If you have to be logical, I'll talk to Suzanna. She knew him a little better. I remember that she knocked him off his motorcycle the first week she had her license."

"I did not knock him off his motorcycle," Suzanna denied, and sank her aching body into a hot, frothy tub. "He fell off his motorcycle when he failed to yield. I had the right-of-way."

"Whatever." Lilah sat on the edge of the tub. "What do we know about him?"

"He has a nasty temper. I thought he was going to murder me that day. He wouldn't have scraped himself all up if he'd been wearing protective gear."

"I mean his background, not his personality."

Weary, Suzanna opened her eyes. Ordinarily the bathroom was the only place she could find true peace and privacy. Now even that had been invaded. "Why?"

"I'll tell you after. Come on, Suze."

"All right, let me think. He was ahead of me in school. Three or four years, I think. Most of the girls were crazy about him because he looked dangerous. His mother was very nice."

"I remember," Lilah murmured. "She came to the house after . . ."

"Yes, after Mom and Dad were killed. She used to do handwork. She'd done some lovely pieces for Mom. We still have some of them, I think. And her husband was a lobsterman. He was lost at sea when we were teenagers. I really don't remember that much."

"Did you ever talk to him?"

"Who, Holt? Not really. He'd sort of swagger around and glare. When we had that little accident he mostly swore at me. Then he went off somewhere — Portland. I remember because Mrs. Marsley was talking about him just the other day when I was selling her some climbing roses. He was a cop for a while, but there was some kind of incident, and he gave it up."

"What kind of incident?"

"I don't know. Whenever she starts I just

let it flow in one ear and on out. I think he's repairing boats or something."

"He never talked about his family with you?"

"Why in the world should he? And why would you care?"

"Because Christian's last name was Bradford, and he had a cottage on the island."

"Oh." Suzanna let out a long breath as she absorbed the information. "Isn't that just our luck?"

Lilah left her sister to soak, and set off to find Max. Before she could go into his room, Coco waylaid her.

"Oh, there you are."

"Darling, you look frazzled." Lilah kissed her cheek.

"And who wouldn't be? That woman . . ." Coco took a deep calming breath. "I'm doing twenty minutes of yoga every morning just to cope. Be a dear and take this in to her."

"What is it?"

"Tonight's menu." Coco set her teeth. "She insists on treating this as though it's one of her cruises."

"As long as we don't have to play shuffleboard."

"Thank you, dear. Oh, did Max tell you his news?"

"Hmm? Oh, yes, belatedly."

"Has he decided? I know it's a wonderful opportunity, but I hate to think he'll be leaving so soon."

"Leaving?"

"If he takes the position, he'll have to go back to Cornell next week. I was going to read the cards last night, but with Aunt Colleen, I just couldn't concentrate."

"What position, Aunt Coco?"

"Head of the history department." She gave Lilah a baffled look. "I thought he'd told you."

"I was thinking of something else." She struggled to keep her voice even. "He's going to leave in a few days?"

"He'll have to decide." Coco cupped a hand under Lilah's chin. "You'll both have to decide."

"He hasn't chosen to bring me in on this one." She stared down at the menu until the words blurred. "It's a terrific opportunity, one I'm sure he's hoped for."

"There are a lot of opportunities in life, Lilah."

She only shook her head. "I couldn't do anything to discourage him from doing something he wants. Not if I loved him. It has to be his decision."

"Who the hell is jabbering out there?"

306

Colleen thumped her cane on the floor.

"I'd like to take that cane and —"

"More yoga," Lilah suggested, forcing a smile. "I'll deal with her."

"Good luck."

"You bellowed, Auntie," Lilah said as she breezed through the door.

"You didn't knock."

"No, I didn't. Tonight's menu, Miss Calhoun. We hope it meets with your approval."

"Little snip." Colleen snatched the paper away, then frowned up at her grandniece. "What's wrong with you, girl? You're white as a sheet."

"Pale skin runs in the family. It's the Irish."

"It's temper that runs in the family." She'd seen eyes that had looked like that before, she thought. Hurt, confused. But then she had been only a child, unable to understand. "Trouble with your young man."

"What makes you say so?"

"Just because I never tied myself down with a man doesn't mean I don't know them. I dallied in my day."

"Dallied." This time the smile came more easily. "A nice word. I suppose some of us are meant to dally through life." She ran a finger down the bedpost. "Just as there are some women men love but don't fall in love with."

"You're jabbering."

"No, I'm trying to be realistic. I'm not usually."

"Realism is cold comfort."

Lilah's brow lifted. "Oh, Lord, I'm afraid I'm more like you than I realized. What a scary thought."

Colleen disguised a chuckle. "Get out of here. You give me a headache. Girl," she said, and Lilah paused at the door, "any man who puts that look into your eyes is worth everything or nothing at all."

Lilah gave a short laugh. "Why, Auntie, you're absolutely right."

She went to his room, but he wasn't there. She'd yet to decide whether to confront Max about his plans or to wait until he told her himself. For better or worse, she thought she would follow her instincts. Idly she picked up a shirt he'd left at the foot of his bed. It was the silly screenprint she'd talked him into on that first shopping trip. The shirt, and the memory, still made her smile. Setting it aside, she crossed to his desk.

He had it piled with books — thick volumes on World War I, a history of Maine, a treatment on the Industrial Revolution. She lifted a brow over a book on fashion in the 1900s. He'd picked up one of the pamphlets from the park that gave a detailed map of the island.

In another pile were the art books. Lilah picked up the top one and opened it to where Max had marked it. As he had, she felt the quick thrill of discovery on reading Christian Bradford's name. Lowering into the chair in front of the typewriter, she read the brief biography twice.

Fascinated, excited, she set the book down to reach for another. It was then she noticed the typed pages, neatly stacked. More reports, she thought with a faint smile. She remembered how tidily he had typed up their interview with Millie Tobias.

*From the top of the high tower of rock, she faced the sea.*

Curious, Lilah settled more comfortably and read on. She was midway through the second chapter when Max came in. Her emotions were so ragged she had to brace before she could speak.

"Your book. You started your book."

"Yeah." He shoved his hands into his pockets. "I was looking for you."

"It's Bianca, isn't it?" Lilah set down the

page she was holding. "Laura — she's Bianca."

"Parts of her." He couldn't have explained how it felt to know that she had read his words — words that had come not so much from his head as from his heart.

"You've set it here, on the island."

"It seemed right." He didn't move toward her, he didn't smile, but only stood looking uncomfortable.

"I'm sorry." The apology was stiff and overly polite. "I shouldn't have read it without asking, but it caught my eye."

"It's all right." With his hands still balled in his pockets, he shrugged. She hated it, he thought. "It doesn't matter."

"Why didn't you tell me?"

"There wasn't really anything to tell. I only have about fifty pages, and it's rough. I thought —"

"It's beautiful." She fought back the hurt as she rose.

"What?"

"It's beautiful," she repeated, and found that hurt turned quickly to anger. "You've got enough sense to know that. You've read thousands of books in your life, and know good work from bad. If you didn't want to share it with me, that's your business."

Still stunned, he shook his head. "It wasn't that I —"

"What was it then? I'm important enough to share your bed, but not to be in on any of the major decisions in your life."

"You're being ridiculous."

"Fine." Rolling easily with her temper, she tossed back her hair. "I'm being ridiculous. Apparently I've been ridiculous for some time now."

The tears crowding her voice confused as much as unnerved him. "Why don't we sit down and talk this through?"

She went with her instincts and shoved the chair at him. "Go ahead. Have a seat. But there's no need to talk anything through. You've started your book, but didn't think it was necessary to mention it. You've been offered a promotion, but didn't consider it worth bringing up. Not to me. You've got your life, Professor, and I've got mine. That's what we said right from the beginning. It's just my bad luck that I fell in love with you."

"If you'd just —" Her last words sank in, dazzling him, dazing him, delighting him. "Oh, God, Lilah." He started to rush forward, but she threw up both hands.

"Don't touch me," she said so fiercely, he stopped, baffled.

311

"What do you expect me to do?"

"I don't expect anything. If I had stuck to that from the beginning, you wouldn't have been able to hurt me like this. As it is, it's my problem. Now, if you'll excuse me."

He grabbed her arm before she reached the door. "You can't say things like this, you can't tell me you're in love with me then just walk away."

"I'll do exactly as I please." Eyes cold, she jerked her arm free. "I don't have anything more to say to you, and there's nothing you can say I want to hear right now."

She walked out of his room into her own and locked the door behind her.

Hours later, she sat in her room, cursing herself for losing her pride and her temper so completely. All she had succeeded in accomplishing was embarrassing herself and Max, and giving herself a vicious headache.

She'd slashed at him, and that had been wrong. She'd pushed him, and that had been stupid. Any hope she'd had of steering him gently into love had been smashed because she'd demanded things he hadn't wanted to give. Now, more than likely, she had ruined a friendship that had been vitally important to her.

There could be no apologizing. No matter how miserable she felt, she couldn't apologize for speaking the truth. And she could never claim to be sorry to have fallen in love.

Restless, she walked out on the terrace. There were clouds over the moon. The wind shoved them across the sky so that the light glimmered for a moment then was smothered. The heat of the day was trapped; the night almost sultry. Fireflies danced over the black carpet of lawn like sparks from a dying fire.

In the distance thunder rumbled, but there was no freshening scent of rain. The storm was out at sea, and even if the capricious wind blew it to land, it might be hours before it hit and relieved the hazy heat. She could smell the flowers, hot and heady, and glanced toward the garden. Her thoughts were so involved that she stared at the glimmer of light for a full minute before it registered.

Not again, she thought, and was almost depressed enough to let the amateur treasure hunters have their thrill. But Suzanna worked too hard on the gardens to have some idiot with a map dig up her perennials. In any case, at least chasing off a trespasser was constructive.

She moved quietly down the steps and into the deeper gloom of the garden. It was simple enough to follow the beam of light. As she walked toward it, Lilah debated whether to use the Calhoun curse or the old The Police Are On Their Way. Both were reliable ways of sending trespassers scurrying. Any other time the prospect might have amused her.

When the light blinked out, she stopped, frowning, to listen. There was only the sound of her own breathing. Not a leaf stirred, and no bird sang in the brush. With a shrug, she moved on. Perhaps they had heard her and had already retreated, but she wanted to be certain.

In the dark, she nearly fell over the pile of dirt. All amusement vanished when her eyes adjusted and she saw the destruction of Suzanna's lovely bed of dahlias.

"Jerks," she muttered, and kicked at the dirt with a sandaled foot. "What the hell is wrong with them?" On a little moan, she bent down to pick up a trampled bloom. Her fingers clenched over it when a hand slapped against her mouth.

"Not a sound." The voice hissed at her ear. Reacting to it, she started to struggle, then froze when she felt the point of the knife at her throat. "Do exactly what I say, and I won't cut you. Try to yell, and I'll slice this across your throat. Understand?"

She nodded and let out a long careful breath when his hand slid away from her mouth. It would have been foolish to ask what he wanted. She knew the answer. But this wasn't some adventure-seeking tourist out for a late-night lark.

"You're wasting your time. The emeralds aren't here."

"Don't play games with me. I've got a map."

Lilah closed her eyes and bit back a hysterical and dangerous laugh.

Max paced his room, scowled at the floor and wished he had something handy to kick. He'd messed things up beautifully. He wasn't exactly sure how he'd managed it, but he'd hurt Lilah, infuriated her and alienated her all in one swoop. He'd never seen a woman go through so many emotions in such a short time. From unhappiness to fury, from fury to frost — hardly letting him get in a single word.

He could have defended himself — if he'd been totally certain of the offense. How could he have known that she'd be offended he hadn't mentioned the book? He hadn't wanted to bore her. No, that was a lie, he admitted. He hadn't told her because he'd been afraid. Plain and simple.

As far as the promotion went, he'd meant to tell her, but it had slipped his mind. How could she believe that he'd have accepted the position and left without telling her?

"What the hell was she supposed to think, you jerk?" he muttered, and plopped down into a chair.

So much for all his careful plans, his step-by-step courtship. His tidy little itinerary for making her fall in love with him had blown up in his face. She'd been in love with him all along.

*She loved him.* He dragged a hand through his hair. Lilah Calhoun was in love with him, and he hadn't had to wave a magic wand or implement any complicated plan. All he'd had to do was be himself.

She'd been in love with him all along, but he'd been too stupid to believe it even when she'd tried to tell him. Now she'd locked herself in her room and wouldn't listen to him.

As far as he could see, he had two choices. He could sit here and wait until she cooled off, then he could beg. Or he could get up right now, beat down her door and demand that she hear him out.

He liked the second idea. In fact, he thought it was inspired.

Without taking the time to debate with himself, he went through the terrace doors. Since it was two in the morning, it made more sense to rattle the glass than beat on the inside door and wake up the household. And it was more romantic. He'd shove open those doors, stride across the room and drag her into his arms until she . . .

His erotic dream veered off as he caught a glimpse of her just before she disappeared into the garden.

Fine, he thought. Maybe better. A sultry garden in the middle of the night. Perfumed air and passion. She wasn't going to know what hit her.

"You know where they are." Hawkins dragged her head back by the hair and she nearly cried out.

"If I knew where they were, I'd have them."

"It's a publicity stunt." He whirled her around, laying the edge of the knife against her cheek. "I figured it out. You've just been playing games to get your names in the paper. I've put time and money into this deal, and it's going to pay off tonight."

She was too terrified to move. Even a tremor might have the blade slicing over her skin. She recognized rage in his eyes, just as she recognized him. This was the man Max had called Hawkins. "The map," she began, then heard Max call her name. Before she could take a breath, the knife was at her throat again.

"Make a sound and I kill you, then him."

He'd kill them both anyway, she thought frantically. It had been in his eyes. "The map," she said in a whisper. "It's a fake." She gasped when the blade pricked her skin. "I'll show you. I can show you where they are."

She had to get him away, away from Max. He was calling her again, and the frustration in his voice had tears welling in her eyes.

"Down that way." She gestured on impulse and let Hawkins drag her down the path until Max's voice faded. At the side edge, the garden gave way to the rocks where the smell and sound of the sea grew stronger. "Over there." She stumbled as he pulled her over the uneven ground. Beside her, the slope ran almost gently to a ridge. Below that, dizzying feet below, were the jagged teeth of rocks and the temperamental sea.

When the first flash of lightning struck, she jolted, then looked desperately over her shoulder. The wind had come up, but she hadn't noticed. The clouds still hid the moon and smothered the light.

Was she far enough away? she wondered. Had Max given up looking for her and gone back inside? Where it was safe.

"If you're trying to pull something on me —"

"No. They're here." She tripped on a jumble of rocks and went down hard. "Under here. In a box under the rocks."

She would inch away slowly, she told herself as every instinct screamed for her to run. While he was involved, she would inch away, then spring up and race to the house. He grabbed the hem of her skirt, ripping it.

"One wrong move, and you're dead." She saw the gleam of his eyes as he bent close. "If I don't find the box, you're dead."

Then his head went up, like a wolf scenting. Out of the dark with a vicious oath, Max leaped.

She screamed then as she saw the wicked edge of the knife glint in the flash of lightning. They hit the ground beside her, rolling over dirt and rock. She was still screaming when she jumped on Hawkins's back to grope for his knife hand. The blade sliced into the ground an inch from Max's face before she was bucked off.

"Damn it, run!" Max shouted at her, gripping Hawkins's beefy wrist with both hands. Then he grunted as a fist grazed his temple.

They were rolling again, the impetus taking them down the slope and onto the ridge. She did run, but toward them, sliding along the loose dirt and sending a shower of pebbles to rain over the struggling bodies. Panting for breath, she grabbed a rock. Her next scream sliced the air as Max's leg dangled over the edge into space.

All he could see was the contorted face above his. All he could hear was Lilah shouting his name. Then he saw stars when Hawkins rammed his head against the rock. For an instant, Max teetered on the edge, the brink between sky and sea. His hand slipped down the sweaty forearm. When the knife came down, he smelled the blood and heard Hawkins's grunt of triumph.

There was something else in the air — something passionate and pleading — as insubstantial as the wind but as strong as bedrock. It slammed into him like a fist. The understanding went through him that he wasn't only fighting for his life, but for Lilah's and the life they would make together.

He wouldn't lose it. With every ounce of strength, he smashed his fist into the face grinning over his. Blood spouted out of Hawkins's nose, then they were grappling again with the knife wedged between them.

Lilah lifted the rock in both hands, started to bring it down when the men at her feet reversed positions. Sobbing, she scrambled back. There were shouts behind her and wild barking. She held tight to the only weapon she had and prayed that she would have the chance to use it.

Then the struggling stopped, and both men went still. With a grunt, Max pushed Hawkins aside and managed to gain his knees. His face was streaked with dirt and blood, his clothes splattered with it. Weakly he shook his head to clear it and looked up at Lilah. She stood like an avenging angel, hair flying, the rock gripped in her hands.

"He rolled on the knife," Max said in a distant voice. "I think he's dead." Dazed, he stared down at his hand, at the dark smear that was the blood of the man he'd killed. Then he looked up at her again. "Are you hurt?"

"Oh, Max. Oh, God." The rock slipped from her fingers as she tumbled to her knees beside him.

"It's okay." He patted her shoulder, stroked her hair. "It's okay," he repeated though he was deathly afraid he would faint.

The dog got there first, then the others came thundering down the slope in nightgowns or robes and hastily pulled-on jeans.

"Lilah." Amanda was there, desperate hands running over her sister's body in a search for wounds. "Are you all right? Are you hurt?"

"No." But her teeth were starting to chatter in the sultry night. "No, he was — Max came." She looked over to see Trent crouched beside him, examining a long gash down his arm. "You're bleeding."

"Not much."

"It's shallow," Trent said between his teeth. "I imagine it hurts like hell."

"Not yet," Max murmured.

Trent looked over as Sloan walked back from the man sprawled on the ridge. Tight-lipped, Sloan shook his head. "It's done," he said briefly.

"It was Hawkins." Max struggled to his feet and stood, swaying. "He had Lilah."

"We'll discuss this later." Her voice uncharacteristically crisp, Coco took Max's good arm. "They're both in shock. Let's get them inside."

"Come on, baby." Sloan reached down to gather Lilah into his arms. "I'll give you a ride home."

"I'm not hurt." From the cradle of his arms she swiveled her head around to look for Max. "He's bleeding. He needs help."

"We'll fix him up," Sloan promised her as they started across the lawn. "Don't you worry, sweetie, the teacher's tougher than you think."

Up ahead, The Towers was ablaze with lights. Another roll of thunder walked the sky above its peaks, then echoed into silence. Abruptly, a tall, thin figure appeared on the second-floor terrace, a cane in one hand, a glinty chrome revolver in the other.

"What the hell is going on around here?" Colleen shouted. "How is a body supposed to get a decent night's sleep with all this hoopla?"

Coco sent one weary glance upward. "Oh, be quiet and go back to bed."

For some reason, Lilah laid her head on Sloan's shoulder and began to laugh.

It was nearly dawn when things settled. The police had come and gone, taking away their grisly package. Questions had been asked and answered — asked and answered again. Lilah had been plied with brandy, fussed over and ordered into a hot bath.

They hadn't let her tend Max's wound. Which might have been for the best, she thought now. Her hands hadn't been steady.

He'd bounced back from the incident remarkably well, she mused as she curled on the window seat in the tower room. While she had still been numb and shaky, he had stood in the parlor, his arm freshly bandaged, and given the investigating officer a clear and concise report of the whole event.

He might have been lecturing one of his classes on the cause and effect of the German economy on World War I, she thought with the ghost of a smile. It had been obvious that Lieutenant Koogar had appreciated the precision and clarity.

Lilah liked to think that her own account had been calm enough, though she hadn't been able to control the trembling very well even when her sisters had joined ranks around her.

Suzanna had finally told the lieutenant

enough was enough and had bundled Lilah upstairs.

But despite the bath and brandy, she hadn't been able to sleep. She was afraid if she closed her eyes that she would see it unfolding again, see Max teetering on the edge of the ridge. They'd hardly spoken since the whole horrible business had happened. They would have to, of course, she reflected. She wanted to clear her thoughts and find just the right words.

But then he walked in, while the sky behind her was being gilded with sunrise, and she was afraid she would never find them.

He stood awkwardly, favoring his left arm, his face shadowed by fatigue. "I couldn't sleep," he began. "I thought you might be up here."

"I guess I needed to think. It's always easier for me to think up here." Feeling as awkward as he, she smoothed back her hair. It fell untamed, the color of the young sun, against the white shoulders of her robe. "Would you like to sit?"

"Yeah." He crossed the room and eased his aching muscles down onto the seat beside her. The silence dragged on, one minute, then two. "Some night," he said at length.

"Yes."

"Don't," he murmured when her eyes filled.

"No." She swallowed them back and stared out at the quiet dawn. "I thought he would kill you. It was like a nightmare — the dark, the heat, the blood."

"It's done now." He took her hand, curled strong fingers around hers. "You led him away from the garden. You were trying to protect me, Lilah. I can't thank you for it."

Off guard, she looked back at him. "What was I supposed to do, let him jump out of the petunias and stab you in the dark?"

"You were supposed to let me take care of you."

She tried to jerk her hand free, but he held firm. "You did, didn't you? Whether I wanted you to or not. You came rushing out like a crazy man, jumping on a maniac with a knife and nearly —" She broke off, struggling for composure while he only sat watching her with those patient eyes. "You saved my life," she said more calmly.

"Then we're even, aren't we?" She shrugged and went back to watching the sky. "The oddest thing happened during those last few minutes I was fighting with Hawkins. I felt myself slipping, losing

326

ground. Then I felt something else, something incredibly strong. I'd say it was simple adrenaline, but it didn't come from me. It was something — other," he said, studying her profile. "I suppose you could call it a force. And I knew that I wasn't meant to lose, that there were reasons I couldn't. I guess I'll always wonder if that force, if that feeling came from you, or from Bianca."

Her lips curved as she looked back at him. "Why, Professor, how illogical."

He didn't smile. "I was coming to your room, to make you listen to me, when I saw you go into the garden. Normally I would consider it only right — or logical — to back off and give you time to recover after what's happened. But things change, Lilah. You're going to listen now."

For a moment she leaned her brow on the cool glass. Then she nodded. "All right, you're entitled. But first I'd like to say that I know I was angry earlier — about the book. It was the wrong reaction —"

"No, it wasn't. You trusted me with a great deal, and I didn't trust you. I was afraid you'd be kind."

"I don't understand."

"Writing's something I've wanted to do

most of my life, but I . . . well, I'm not used to taking risks."

She had to laugh and, going with instinct, leaned over to kiss the bandage on his arm. "Max, what a thing to say now of all times."

"I haven't been used to taking risks," he corrected. "I thought if I told you about the book and got up the courage to show you a few pages, you'd see it as a pipe dream and be kind."

"It's stupid to be so insecure about something you have such talent for." Then she sighed. "And it was stupid for me to take it so personally. Take it from someone who isn't particularly kind. It's going to be a wonderful book, Max. Something you can be very proud of."

He cupped a hand behind her neck. "Let's see if you say that after I make you read several hundred more pages." He leaned toward her, touched his lips gently to hers. But when he started to deepen the kiss, she jumped up.

"I'll give you the first critique when it's published." Nerves humming, she began to pace.

"What is it, Lilah?"

"Nothing. So much has happened." She took a deep breath before she turned, smile firmly in place. "The promotion. I was so involved with myself before that I didn't even congratulate you."

"I wasn't keeping it from you."

"Max, let's not go over all of that again. The important thing is it's a wonderful honor. I think we should have a party to celebrate before you go."

A smile ghosted around his mouth. "Do you?"

"Of course. It isn't every day you get made head of your department. The next thing you know, you'll be dean. It's only a matter of time. And then —"

"Lilah, sit down. Please."

"All right." She clung to the desperate gaiety. "We'll have Aunt Coco bake a cake, and —"

"You're happy about the offer then?" he interrupted.

"I'm very proud of you," she said, and brushed the hair from his brow. "I like knowing that the powers that be appreciate how valuable you are."

"And you want me to accept?"

Her brows drew together. "Of course. How could you refuse? This is a wonderful opportunity for you, something you've worked for and earned."

"That's a pity." He shook his head and

leaned back, still watching her. "I've already declined."

"You did what?"

"I declined, with appreciation. It's one of the reasons I never mentioned the whole business to you. I didn't see it as an issue."

"I don't understand. A career opportunity like this isn't something you casually turn aside."

"It depends on your career. I also tendered my resignation."

"You — you quit? But that's crazy."

"Yes, probably." And because it was, he had to grin. "But if I went back to Cornell to teach, the book would end up in a file somewhere gathering dust." He held out his hand, palm up. "You looked at this once and told me I'd have to make a choice. I've made it."

"I see," she said slowly.

"You only see part of it." He glanced around the tower. The light was pearly now, slowly going gold. There couldn't be a better time or a better place. He took both of her hands.

"I've loved you from the first moment I saw you. I couldn't believe that you could ever feel the same way, no matter how much I wanted it. Because I didn't, I made things more difficult than they might have been. No, don't say anything, not yet. Just listen." He pressed their joined hands to his lips. "You've changed me. Opened me. I know that I was meant to be with you, and if it took deceit and a necklace that's been lost the best part of a century, then that's what it had to take. Whether or not we'll ever find the emeralds, they brought you to me, and you're all the treasure I'll ever need."

He brought her close to kiss her mouth as morning rose and washed the last shadows from the room.

"I don't want this to be a dream," she murmured. "I've sat here before thinking of you, wishing for this."

"This is real." He framed her face then kissed her again to prove it.

"You're all I want, Max. I've been looking for you for such a long time." Gently she combed her fingers through the hair on his brow. "I was so afraid you wouldn't love me back, that you'd go away. That I'd have to let you go away."

"This has been home since the first night. I can't explain it."

"You don't have to."

"No." He turned his lips into her palm. "Not to you. One last thing." Again he took her hands. "I love you, Lilah, and I have to ask if you're willing to take the risk of marrying an unemployed former teacher who thinks he can write a book."

"No." She smiled and linked her arms around his neck. "But I'm going to marry a very talented and brilliant man who is writing a wonderful book."

With a laugh, he rested his brow on hers. "I like your way better."

"Max." She snuggled into the crook of his arm. "Let's go tell Aunt Coco. She'll be so thrilled she'll fix us blueberry pancakes for an engagement breakfast."

He eased her back against the pillows. "How about an engagement brunch?"

She laughed and flowed into the kiss. "This time I like your way better."

The employees of Thorndike Press hope you have enjoyed this Large Print book. All our Thorndike and Wheeler Large Print titles are designed for easy reading, and all our books are made to last. Other Thorndike Press Large Print books are available at your library, through selected bookstores, or directly from us.

For information about titles, please call:

(800) 223-1244

or visit our Web site at:

www.gale.com/thorndike
www.gale.com/wheeler

To share your comments, please write:

Publisher
Thorndike Press
295 Kennedy Memorial Drive
Waterville, ME   04901